GIRLING

THE DRIFTLESS UNSOLICITED NOVELLA SERIES

• • • • • • • • • • •

Technologies of the Self	Haris A. Durrani
Faith Healer	Victoria G. Smith
Girling	C. Kubasta
Rosa	Barbara de la Cuesta

The Driftless Unsolicited Novella Series

GIRLING

C. Kubasta

Brain Mill Press

Green Bay, Wisconsin

Published in the United States by Brain Mill Press.
Print ISBN 978-1-942083-87-0
EPUB ISBN 978-1-942083-90-0
MOBI ISBN 978-1-942083-88-7
PDF ISBN 978-1-942083-89-4

Cover art: "Warm Ways" by Janelle Cordero.
© Janelle Cordero.
Cover design by Ampersand Book Design.

www.brainmillpress.com

Published by Brain Mill Press, the Driftless Unsolicited Novella Series publishes those novellas selected as winners of the Driftless Unsolicited Novella Contest each year.

for Carmen, of course

The seeming statement of recognition "It's a girl!"
is thus an interpellation which initiates the process
of "girling," an assignment never to be fully com-
pleted because "femininity" is "the forcible cita-
tion of a norm" and not a pre-existing reality.

—Cristina Bacchilega,
*Postmodern Fairy Tales:
Gender and Narrative Strategies*

• • •

I was always in your context.
—Tracey Knapp, *Mouth*

CONTENTS

GIRLING

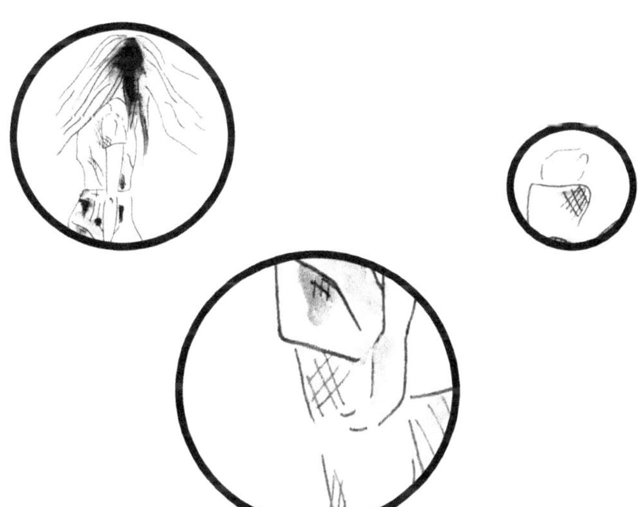

ONE
THE CALICO RULE

Kate had never seen a kitten being born. She wasn't sure she should—that her parents would approve of this new knowledge, this experiential learning. She didn't even know Sadie was going to have kittens. Usually Sadie cat was outside all the time, unless it was really cold in winter, and then she was only allowed into the house as far as the kitchen. Once Kate and Mollie snuck her up into the bedroom to sleep, but Sadie kept scratching at the door all night, so Mollie opened the window and Sadie went out onto the roof and disappeared.

"Kate!" Mollie yelled, "hurry!"

Kate and Sarah ran to the mud room, and Kate skittered to the floor in front of Sadie's nest of rags and castoff blankets while Sarah whispered "Shh!" and gave Mollie a stern look. Next to Sadie was a little wet white lump, with an orange spot.

"Is that a kitten?" Kate asked.

"Mm-hmm," Aunt Sarah answered as she picked up the lump and wiped it down. She wiped it kind of hard and dug around the edges until the lump had a face and stretched open its mouth. She put the lump with the face up by Sadie's face and Sadie started licking it.

"Here comes another one!" Mollie whisper-yelled, and Kate looked near Sadie's tail where a trail of slime and another lump seemed to be pushing out. It was another white wet lump, but this one had a big black mark that curved around it. As it was coming out, Sadie stopped licking the first kitten and went still, and her eyes locked onto Kate's, but not like she was really looking at her. Aunt Sarah cleaned it off, and it joined the other one, rubbing and mewling next to its mother.

There were two more. The third was bigger than the others, but no matter how much Aunt Sarah worked on it, it never started moving. She set it next to Sadie for a minute, but the cat sniffed it and turned away, and Aunt Sarah picked it up and put it in the garbage can on the porch. When she saw Kate watching her, she said, "Stillborn."

"It happens, Kate. I showed it to Sadie, so she'd know, and then I put it away."

"Shouldn't we bury it?"

Aunt Sarah gave her a little hug. "That's sweet, Katie. But that kitten was never alive. And Sadie's got a lot of work to do with her three little ones." The last kitten born was much smaller than the other two. It was three colors, just like Sadie. Mollie said it was the "runt." She said it would have to work hard to get strong like its brother and sister, but if it could get strong it would be all right. Already the other two kittens were piling over the runt, quicker to Sadie's belly; even blind, they crawled over it like just another wadded-up piece of cloth.

Aunt Sarah watched Kate watch the kittens. "I've got a lot of work to do to make dinner for my own little ones tonight," she said, "and I don't think Uncle RJ will have time to make a kitten funeral either."

She and Mollie had been deep in Mollie's closet, building a cave of blankets when Uncle RJ knocked at the door. "Girls," he said, "Sadie's having kittens…" and Mollie grabbed her hand and they went down to the mudroom. Sadie cat was a calico, curled in the bed of fabric, her fur moving quick, breathing hard. Aunt Sarah had set up a hot lamp over the nest and told the girls to be quiet and watch. After watching for what seemed forever, Kate had wandered back into the kitchen where Aunt Sarah was stirring a big pot of spaghetti sauce for dinner, and the strainer in the sink held elbow macaroni topped with big pats of butter.

"Any kittens yet?" Sarah asked.

"No," Kate mumbled, "nothing's happening," and she picked up the shaker of cheese and shook it to loosen the clumps stuck in the bottom.

"Well," Sarah said, "it takes some time, but she's definitely started. Whenever Sadie cat's ready for kittens she goes to that spot and makes her bed. If you wait a little bit longer, you'll get to see the kittens being born."

• • •

Mollie was Kate's best friend and cousin, and she lived up on the ridge outside of town. Nearly every weekend Kate would spend a night at Mollie's, with her Uncle RJ and Aunt Sarah and Mollie's brothers. The weekend days were wide open—Uncle RJ tinkering in the garage, Aunt Sarah in the kitchen, and the kids somewhere or other in the house or the woods all day until dinner time. In the summer, they'd walk through the woods to the ridgeline, and over the ridge was a pond. If it was just Kate and Mollie, they'd wiggle out of their clothes and swim—Mollie called it "skinny-dipping"—up where the trees grew thick by the water and they could pretend there was no one around for miles. After, they'd shriek and run back down the path in the woods, clothes sticking to wet skin, pretending to be chased until they got back to the house where they'd warm up in the kitchen while Aunt Sarah cooked a big dinner. She'd make them hot cocoa even in summer, with little marshmallows, and brush the lanks of their wet hair, picking leaves and pine needles from the tangles, sighing, wondering "what they got into," and laughing as they squirmed. The boys were older and never around, and whenever the girls got near her lap Aunt Sarah would hold them tight, keeping them planted there longer than they could stand. The pots on the stove boiled and steamed and spit.

As Kate grew up, the kitchen at Aunt Sarah and Uncle RJ's would figure heavily in much of her imagining—in some of her favorite stories, stories that centered around a normal-seeming house fraught with secrets, it was always that kitchen she pictured: the wide-open space in the front room bordered by the long table with extra chairs always ready for visitors; the way the morning light poured in from the back garden; the small area of cupboards that never had enough space to hold everything; the old fireplace they never used, except for the hearth that made the perfect bench for sitting. And there were the side rooms—one full of junk piled high to the ceiling that just might be treasure, one piled with sewing projects that never seemed to get finished, the mudroom always housing Sadie and some litter of kittens.

That trail through the woods became the Ur-trail through the Ur-woods—the woods filled with paths to stay on, paths to stray from. And Uncle RJ, still, was the clearest picture of what a father who loved his daughter looked like—he had so much love it spilled over to his daughter's friends. After Kate and Mollie were no longer friends, barely cousins, it was Uncle RJ who seemed most sad, who would still call to see how Kate was, and talk on the phone, pretending it was Mollie who wanted to know how she was doing, how school was, if she was liking swimming lessons, if she was excited about her new teacher. The first time her mom handed her the phone, she said, "It's Mollie," but it wasn't. After that, Mom would call her to the phone and mouth "Uncle RJ" and Kate would take the call in the kitchen while her mother cleaned up after dinner, listening with one ear.

• • •

The night the kittens were born, they ate macaroni and spaghetti sauce with garlicky bread, and Kate kept getting up to check on the kittens and Sadie. All night the little lumps of fur lay curled under the heat lamp in the nest of blankets, the kittens pawed up to Sadie's belly. Sadie's purr was loud and deep, and the kittens made little mewling sounds. Kate would reach out to touch one of the kittens nursing, and one of Sadie's eyes would open and watch her. She hissed once.

Over the next few weeks, whenever she got to Mollie's, she'd look for the kittens first. They were wobbly and blind, bumping into everything, paws all over each other. The runt got bigger, and soon the only way she could tell it was the runt was because it looked most like Sadie, with orange and brown and black. The white-and-orange kitten was another girl. The white-and-black kitten was a boy and looked like the white-and-black tom that roamed the top of the ridge that Mollie said was Sadie's boy-friend.

Most calico cats are females. There's a link between the genes for coloration—especially the orange/non-orange color—and the X chromosome. Even if Aunt Sarah hadn't known how to sex the kittens, she could have guessed that the runt—three-colored, like Sadie—would have been another girl. Rarely, a male cat has three colors, but they're usually sickly or sterile, or both. In any case, both Mollie and Kate tried to inspect the kittens to see what Aunt Sarah found when she looked, but couldn't tell what they were looking for, not on kittens. They didn't know about the calico rule either, but knew that they both looked like their mothers—everyone said so. Mollie knew how to make dinners already and sew a straight seam; she knew how to tell when her dad was looking for a fight. Kate knew things too, that her mother knew, but didn't know yet that there would come a time she'd worry that she'd become her mother. That that was something girls inherited from their mothers too—along with the color of their hair, and other things hidden on chromosomes, discovered only lately, under close inspection.

• • •

Cousin Mollie moved away when they were in fifth grade. Kate thought they'd still see each other—maybe at Christmas—but they were too far away, and the next time was in eighth grade, when Mollie's older brother got married. But Mollie had new friends and even brought a boyfriend to the wedding as her "date," and they barely talked or said hello at all. Uncle RJ and Aunt Sarah had gotten divorced, and Kate didn't really understand if Uncle RJ was still her uncle or if Aunt Sarah was still her aunt. They were both there for their son's wedding, and they both hugged her and told her how pretty she looked and how she was growing up, but Kate couldn't remember who was still her family and who she was supposed to love—and who was ex-family and she was only supposed to be polite to.

On the drive home, she was telling her mom about Sadie's kittens.

"You never told me about that," Mom said, "but I think a lot of things happened at Mollie's I didn't know about…" and she smiled. Kate thought about the skinny-dipping, but also finding Uncle RJ's magazines, and kissing Mollie's brother—the one who got married tonight.

There were times when she woke up at Mollie's and heard angry voices and thought they were Uncle RJ and Aunt Sarah. Once when she nudged Mollie's shoulder to ask about it, she was already awake. "Just ignore it, stupid," Mollie said, and she sounded really angry. Kate rolled over to the far edge of the bed and wedged herself between the mattress and the wall. She wanted a pillow to pile on top of her head to drown out the sounds, but Mollie had them all, and they were stuffed around her ears and her face, but what little part of her face was showing was all red and streaky.

Once when she closed the door to the upstairs bathroom, she saw the hole behind the towel where the wall was all crumbly. She asked Mollie about it, and Mollie rolled her eyes at Kate and told her to shut up. After that, she never asked stupid questions, and if she and Mollie came running down the hill and heard Aunt Sarah and Uncle RJ yelling at each other in the garage, they turned and ran back into the woods, pretending they were playing another game until everything became quiet again.

"Mom," Kate said, "Sadie always had kittens—don't you remember?"

"Well, I remember RJ taking care of the kittens…" her mom said, and there was an edge to her voice. That's right, Kate remembered, RJ was her mom's brother. Uncle RJ was still her uncle.

"Uncle RJ didn't take care of the kittens," Kate answered. "Sadie did most of the work, but I only remember Aunt Sarah helping." Someone should stand up for Aunt Sarah. She would have added, *And Mollie, and me,* but her mom interrupted.

"That's not what I meant, Katie. What do you think happened to all those kittens?"

"They went to new homes." She remembered how after that first time, there were always kittens. Sadie never got "fixed"—that's what her mom called it, and that black-and-white tomcat was always around. She and Mollie got older and the kittens weren't so interesting anymore, but there were always kittens, and then the kittens were gone, and Mollie and Aunt Sarah would always say that they went to new homes.

"Their new home was a sack with a few rocks in it, courtesy of your Uncle RJ. He threw them into the pond."

Kate felt all the breath go out of her lungs. She thought about Uncle RJ, who had spent too much time at the bar at the wedding tonight and, slurring, asked Kate to dance. She was embarrassed, but Aunt

Sarah walked up and smiled and took RJ's arm, and it was almost, for a minute, like they were still married. The way Sarah held his arm was like just before or just after a fight. And the way RJ looked at Sarah anybody could see his eyes were wet, and it didn't have anything to do with his son getting married.

Kate knew her mother was watching her, even as she pretended to be watching the road. She thought about the skinny-dipping pond, in the quiet of the trees, where she and Mollie thought no one ever came. She thought of their feet ripping open the bags, stepping on the rocks, the little skeletons of rib cages and skulls.

They were waiting at the stop sign to turn onto Main.

"What about Floozy's puppies?" Floozy was Mollie's golden retriever, and when she had puppies she took over the garage, behind the table where Uncle RJ kept the drawer of magazines. But Kate couldn't be there when Floozy had her puppies—no one could. For a week after, if anyone tried to go into that part of the garage, the dog would charge, snarling and barking. After a few weeks, the puppies would venture out themselves, and then Floozy must have decided it was safe.

"Mom, what about the puppies?" But her mom didn't say anything, just kept craning her neck back and forth, looking for a break in the line of cars.

"It's always so hard to make this left turn off of Townline," she said.

• • •

When Kate first saw the kittens with their eyes open they were bright blue. They started to play and move a little farther away from Sadie, and Sadie didn't hiss anymore when Kate picked them up.

And then the kittens were gone. Kate went and pet Sadie for a long time, thinking she might be lonely. Sadie purred loudly at the petting, but when Kate tried to pick her up and hold her, she put her claws out and left a big red scratch down Kate's arm that dripped a little bit of blood. Kate pulled her sleeves down to hide the scratch, and since no one else mentioned the kittens, neither did she.

TWO

THE SCRIMSHANDER

Whether she is the Miller's Daughter, or the Farmer's Daughter, or the Sheepherder's Daughter, now she is the Princess, soon to become a Queen. To become the Queen, she must fill these three rooms, with only the work of her own hands and her own body, but she knows not the skills needed to fill these rooms from floorboards to rafters. She suspects, as all newly-to-be-wed must suspect, that she has somehow arrived here by accident—that she will never be able to accomplish the tasks before her.

Their kingdom will be a kingdom of the air. There has been a falling out with the old King—and the only gifts bequeathed on their wedding day will be cold lumps of gold, and stores of future gold for the heirs. These will be put into trust, but the old King and Queen will not attend them on this day—they will not bless the new Queen in her wedding finery, or assist her before she walks down the aisle to her betrothed. Perhaps if the Old Queen were there, she could offer some guidance for how to fill the three rooms that wait empty for her hand, her talents, her desiring. Her own mother is no help—she sat idly by while her father bartered her to the Prince come looking for a bride. No one will tell her what was promised—what it was she was supposed to be able to make or do.

There has been a great un-naming in the distant past. When the Prince asks for her hand, he tells her that it will be she and he, and they will take to the air, leaving the land behind for the Old King and Queen who have cast them out. "Yes," he says, "I have parents, but they have disowned me. Yes," he says, "I have brothers and sisters, but they will not own me, afraid of my parents' displeasure."

"And what of our future children?" she asks.

"They must make their own way," he answers, "in our new Kingdom." She nods and smiles, to be chosen by such a man, whose grin cracks the sun-bleached skin he wears like pleasure on his thin frame—who promises joy with his horse-laugh and easy ways.

But when she asks what to do with the three empty rooms, he pretends she is joking, that of all the half-jests and jokes, surely this is the one answer she knows.

He talks in his sleep: *First you must feather the nest. First you must make us the means to escape.*

In the first room is a walking-foot sewing machine, hammers and nails, foam and finest leathers, cording, glue and steam machines. There is unspun wool and meshing and heavy thread. When he shows her his flying machines, his fingers trail along the edges of seats, cup the rounds of foot beds, of consoles and machine panels. All blue metal, the unburnished shine of aluminum and rivet. She must upholster this Kingdom of the Air—create a home in the home left to him after his rightful home has been taken from him. It takes years, the blood of her fingers, the crimping of her bones, but she makes him a place where even free from the land of the Old King, he can rest his head in the handiwork of her hours and know he is loved.

But the second room and the third room are empty of everything. When she walks in those rooms she only hears her footfalls on the floor, sees the patterned light through glass panes.

Once Upon a Time, three erstwhile cousins saved a Queen from a lifetime of spinning. They paraded their ugliness before the King: the broad foot, the hanging lip, the broad thumb. When he asked, diplomatically, how they came to be so ugly, they replied, "from spinning." From spinning. The new Queen shows the King her hands, the damage from upholstering the Kingdom of the Air. *Here is where the leather ripped the nail from its root. Here is where the hammer fell, purpling the nail. Here is where the needle pierced the nail and through the finger, reminding me of its power.*

It takes nine months, but she learns how to fill the other two rooms. They are filled with her own blood and bone. The first child squalls, but her hair is soft as floss. The King names her Ann, a hiding. Derived from Hannah, it means, "God has favored me with a child." The King hopes hiding will keep her safe. The new Queen wonders what all the hiding is for—who are they hiding from? They have already retreated from the Kingdom, from any birthright beyond that already given. She wonders too why the King briefly touches the child, then turns away. The birth was hard, hours and hours of pain that she thought she wouldn't see the end of. Again she wished for a mother—any mother—to take her by the hand and explain each pain, each moment of wonder and despair. Briefly she remembers the King talking to someone else, hearing, "No, it's a girl," but when she asked who else attended the birth, her husband lied and said no one.

Again she wonders: who are they hiding from?

Fathers believe in the magic of names; they beg and beck from the begats the promise of patrimony secured. First and last, pat.

Mothers know children are scrimshawed from their very bones; the leisure hours between danger. Here, hollowness—here, layering ossification, here calcium fragments and broken bits left from the tumble-me-down. The child is made in ambergris, fingernails first.

Two years later, the second room is claimed, and the boy is born in pain, with hair soft as floss. The King gives him his own name and they take to the Kingdom of the Air, always hiding from something, from someone, but she never knows who.

The Scrimshander's bones are covered with pictograph narratives, etched almost to translucence. The second birth dislocated her tailbone; to bear her own weight, let alone someone else's, is unbearable.

There is the business of names. It matters what the children are called. The King spends days and nights with great tomes of names, searching for one. When she tells him she cannot have another child, his eyes are soft. "Do not worry, my Queen, I will not ask that of you." But he is always looking for some name.

The second child was harder coming than the first, and the woman who held her hand at the end told her she would not fill any more rooms. She had no more blood and bone to knit a new child with. "Care for this one," she said, "keep him safe." The Queen felt warned, admonished.

• • •

But she cannot; she did not. Ann grows strong, but with long shadows under her eyes, a tight smile—she is always playing at names, making guessing games of difficult names. At three, her son grows shadows too, but they lengthen without end. The Kingdom of the Air is not large enough—they must touch down here and there, and always there is some reminder of the Old King and Queen who will not know these new children, these new sorrows.

The damage done to a mother who loses her child is both visible and invisible. Here the eyelid droops, crepe and sallow. Here the lips thin. Here the liver pickles, drenched in the bile that replaces her very blood.

She becomes a watcher, scanning the horizon over the River of Grass—the saw grass sedge that layers this land. It bends graceful in the wind—to walk with the bend is easy, all soft current. But to turn back and return bloodies the skin; serrated edges bite and burn. Instead she waits and watches for the silver glint of wings, listens for the drone of engine, the swoop and glide of graceful arc. It is the new Queen's toil to wait and watch, to log and record, a record of portents and harbingers.

The new King and Queen take to staring at each other, across tables, across quiet rooms. Each room has its own kind of silence—the silence of straining to be quiet, the silence of quiet when there is nothing to say, the silence of quiet that hides crying, the silence of quiet that hides crying that has ceased. Ann has learned to be quiet too—to hear the slap of playing cards always dealing solitaire, the wind-chime music of a tonic that can never soothe, the click of tumbler and locks when a door closes trying not to be heard.

Ann plays in a playhouse behind the hangar, with her dolls lined up in their beds. At night, she sleeps in her own room; the planks quieted by rugs, the sunlight-through-panes dampened by curtains. Charlie's room is again empty.

THREE

·········

RUNNING AWAY

First Kate stole the can opener. It was the first tool they figured they'd need after they began stealing cans of food and realized they had no way to open them. They had a can of tomatoes, two cans of corn, some chicken soup, and something called "cannellini" that just looked like regular chili beans, but white. Kate had added artichoke hearts to the pile, but Robbie made her put it back in the pantry. He didn't like artichoke hearts anyway, and he was older and he was in charge. They were making good progress on the plan, he thought, but then Kate asked how they were going to open the cans and they realized they needed a can opener.

The kitchen junk drawer was full of all sorts of useful things—too full. Dad was always complaining that he couldn't find anything, and could barely get it shut or get it open, so they liberated an extra pair of scissors, two bent forks, a roll of duct tape, and a spool of thread with pins and a needle stuck in the top. They added this to the can opener and hid all the supplies in the back basement behind the pile of scrap wood thick with a layer of wood shavings and the little brown pellets Robbie said were mouse turds.

They planned to take Dad's scooter when it was time to go.

Robbie was twelve, and Kate didn't understand why he wanted to run away, but he asked her to come along and she said yes because she loved him and would have said yes to anything he asked her to do. He said they could live in the marsh behind his friend Andy's house—Andy's family owned acres and acres of land, and no one ever went back into the marsh. Robbie and Andy had been playing back there one day and found an old house, with broken-out windows but a pretty good floor and a roof that was mostly whole, and Robbie said Andy could keep a secret. Robbie said it would be like camping, something they did weekends in the summer. Mom and Dad and Robbie and Kate and their little brother Jake would load up the van and head north. They'd canoe all day Saturday and cook over the campfire for dinner and breakfast, and go swimming with a bar of soap when it was time to clean up. Kate would sit in the front of one canoe, but Robbie knew how to steer already, and he could build a fire all by him-self and Kate knew how to cook scrambled eggs, so they figured they could live for quite a while in the house with broken-out windows. Especially if they had a can opener.

Robbie had started taking money from the top drawer of Dad's dresser, just a little bit at a time. Dad kept his poker money there, next to the socks that Mom paired and turned the tops over on to keep together. It was mostly quarters, but if there was a good night, there'd be lots of bills. When Dad played poker, he called it "Bible Study" so that he could keep going during Lent. He played with the doctor who delivered all the kids, and the Phy Ed teacher from the middle school, and a few men he knew from work. When "Bible Study" was at the house, Mom would make lots of snacks, and even though it was a party the kids all had to go to bed early. Mom said it was an *adult party* and there'd be *inappropriate language* and *other shenanigans* and it *wasn't safe for young ears*. Robbie said it wasn't really stealing because they'd use the money to buy milk and eggs from the grocery store in the next town when they needed it, and gas for the scooter. And they wouldn't have to go to school anymore, and they'd be busy gathering firewood for cooking and to get ready for the winter because the house with the broken-out windows wouldn't keep them warm once the snow fell.

Kate worried about missing school, but she worried more about disappointing Robbie. During the summer, they'd spend long days outside, building a fort of scrap wood in the big maple, nailing pieces of wood for ladder rungs up the trunk before they could get to the forked place to make a floor. They never seemed to finish the fort. The ladder rungs always broke off or shredded under their feet. Just when they'd get two or three boards together for the floor, it'd cant to one side or the other, and they'd have to tear it all out and start again. Kate never got to hang the dishrag curtains she meant to put over the windows—because there never were windows to hang curtains on. The fort-making became a summers-long project. The maple grew scars up and down its long, wide trunk, and now Robbie was talking about how they could collect the sap and make syrup from the sticky that leaked from all their nail holes.

Mom said they *were going to kill that tree* when she came out to call them in for dinner. The later afternoon light would be slanting through the leaves and Dad would be late coming home, as he usually was, as he and his work friends had to meet for the "Five O'Clock Club" before they went home to their families—but Dad was the only one with a family, and no one else really wanted to go home, so sometimes the nights would go later and later, and the dinner would be done and all the dishes washed and all the kids in pajamas before they heard the sound of Dad's car in the garage and the door swinging open, its pneumatic shriek.

• • •

When school started in the fall, Robbie was in junior high and he barely talked to Kate anymore. When she walked toward him on the bus, he'd turn away and pretend he didn't see her, and she'd have to sit quickly in one of the front seats so he didn't see she was hurt. But when he'd asked her if she wanted to run away, she didn't ask for any details, she just said "yes," because his asking was like the morning sun when they went out with hammers to unbend the re-collected nails and start again on the tree fort, possibility stretched out over the long days of summer. It was like the start of dinner when they went in to sit at the table with the five plates and napkins and waited, but pretended they weren't waiting, to see if Dad would be home in time to eat.

It was like the time he brought her a squirrel he'd killed with the shotgun and asked her to clean it and pick all the lead and even though she hated the job she'd done it really well—gotten almost every piece of birdshot. Afterward, Robbie had said that her "girl hands" were "good for something after all" and she'd been proud. And that's when he'd asked her to run away.

"How long will we be gone?" she finally asked him one day, when they were in the basement, adding a ball of twine to the pile. Robbie had found it in the barn, in the hayloft.

Robbie didn't answer, but he looked at her quick, over his shoulder, and she knew she shouldn't have asked.

She stuck out her foot and toed the pile of canned goods. "How are we going to haul all of this there?"

"It'll fit," he said. "There's the two baskets, and your backpack and my backpack."

"What about clothes and blankets?" She pictured the scooter loaded down already with the hoard of food, and both of them, riding double. Robbie said they'd take the back roads by the farms, where the only people who would see them were the migrants coming in from the pickle fields.

"We'll both put on all of our clothes, in layers." Robbie had it all planned. "If we meet here right after school, we'll have time for maybe two or three trips before anyone gets home."

Another time she asked, "What if we get caught?"

"We'll stay out behind Andy's for a few months, until things die down," Robbie said. "Until they stop looking for us."

When Robbie said this, he sounded happy, but Kate hadn't thought that Mom and Dad would ever stop looking for them. But the way Robbie said it, he sounded very sure. Even though he was only twelve, the four years between them meant he may as well have been another adult.

• • •

When Robbie started seventh grade, he asked Kate to do his spelling homework. She loved it—the words were harder, but she really liked the challenge problems at the end, when she could guess what other words could be made with the letters of the assigned words—she rearranged letters for hours, looking them up in the Scrabble dictionary until she'd finished a whole page. When Robbie came home the next day, he threw a balled-up piece of paper at Kate's head. "Thanks a lot," he said, angry. When she undid the piece of paper, she saw a big red "F" at the top. "My teacher knew I cheated, smartass, because you did the extra cred-it." He didn't talk to her for three days.

Once she asked about their little brother. Robbie said they had to leave him behind—he was too little to help, and they had to leave at least one kid for their mom.

There might have been other reasons they didn't go, but Kate remembers asking her mom what she'd do if Kate ever ran away. Mom was ironing in the basement, a big stack of Dad's button-down shirts, and Kate was on the floor, bored, because Robbie was gone with his friends for the day and Jake was taking his nap. She heard the iron stop, and the cool basement was very quiet.

"What, Kate?" her mom asked, as she grabbed the can of spray starch and shook it.

"I was just wondering…I mean, if I ran away, would you keep my room the way it is?"

Kate loved her room. It was the biggest kid's room in the house—her dad always said the girl needed the biggest room—and she had a big bed with a canopy. The bedspread and the canopy were blue gingham, and the wallpaper was Holly Hobby, and her doll collection was nestled on the shelves across from the wall, smiling down at her. She had bookshelves and bookshelves of books and a big closet full of dresses, and on her dresser she had a bottle of perfume called *Tatiana!* that Robbie had bought her for a present last Christmas.

"Well, we'd probably keep your room for a little while, but then, if you were gone and not coming back, we'd probably change it," Mom said. She was working the iron's pointed tip around the buttons on Dad's shirt, pushing the button that made the steam spit out. The iron made a click-click-click noise every time it hit a button.

Kate tried to see her mom's face, to see if she was joking, to see if she knew why Kate was asking—if she knew that Kate was really asking, that she and Robbie were really planning on running away. She tried to look out of the corner of her eye without turning her face, because her face felt as hot as the iron's steam spout clicking on the buttons on Dad's shirt. Her mom had taught her to turn the shirts inside out—that way the iron doesn't hit the buttons, or get stuck, or work loose the thread holding them on.

"I do need a sewing room," Mom continued, "instead of always working down in this basement…" Kate headed up the stairs before her mom could see her face.

Later that night, at dinner, there were five plates and napkins, but only Mom and Kate and her baby brother were home to eat. Robbie had called from Andy's and stayed there and didn't get home until late, and when Kate ran into him in the hallway on her way to bed she blurted out, "I'm not going."

• • •

It was late spring and school would be over soon, but that summer they didn't work much on the maple-tree fort. Robbie would have Andy over to help instead, and pretty soon there was enough of a floor that the two of them stood on it and threw rocks at Kate and Jake when they tried to cross the front lawn. Nobody got hit, but Kate could hear the heavy thunk the rocks made when they landed next to her, hitting the sugar sand, and both she and Jake were crying and zigging and zagging all over the lawn. Finally Kate ran to Jake and picked him up and they ran to the garage. When she looked back, Robbie wasn't even watching her, but Andy was standing with a big rock in his hand, ready. Kate scraped the sand and snot from her little brother's face and took him into the house. In the bathroom, she ran the water until it got warm and gently cleaned him with a washcloth, trying to soothe him. It's what her mother would have done.

When she finally worked up the courage to check on the pile in the back basement there was nothing there anyway, but she never asked Robbie about it, and he never mentioned it again. In a few years, Mom would run away, or at least that's what Dad said, so that's what Robbie said too, and when Kate and her little brother would go for their half-time at Mom's house Robbie would stay behind at Dad's anyway.

FOUR

· · · · · · · ·
BEFORE KATE

The aerial view would make the saw grass look soft, like undulating waves. It's only when she walks through it that it becomes teeth. The wind blows, and the stems soften and bend, arcing over, burying. The patterns of palm and bark and scrub disappear, so all appears like the postcards, rimmed with beaches and blue waves, the arterials of highways and overpasses. Even the St. Augustine grass, densely matted, escapes the suggestion of touch, appearing only uniform green.

At ground level, the she knows that things aren't always what they seem. The family of three has closed around its own wound, slowly collapsed, and now looks photograph perfect. Here's the perfect sandy-blond daughter, her shoulder-length hair, her skipping legs and feet in her white Keds and ankle socks. Here's the tall, tan father, who pilots the skies, eyes always on the horizon, the dip of blue into blue. Here's the comfort-mother, who sews the eyelet-dresses, the corded-edged cushions for the airplanes, the valances and panels for the home she makes home in. It's only when Ann walks that she knows the saw grass has teeth.

Next year will be a year of changes—she will be going to a new school. She has outgrown the salt-spalled and blistered elementary in their neighborhood, where she learned to tie her shoes, to read her letters, to follow with her finger, tracing first the simple words on the page, then later the longer ones, learning the stories about families and the things they do together, learning later how to stand, shyly, at Show and Tell, and tell her own stories. She learned how to read people's faces, how the first time she mentioned Charlie being sick her teacher rushed over the ends of her words, how she carried a note home from school in her backpack, how her mother had to explain that some things were *family stories*, things she didn't need to share.

Now at the dining room table, the round table with just three chairs, her parents talked incessantly about where she'd go to school next year. The school where most of her friends were going was not where she would be going. The reason must have been one of those things that didn't need to be shared, because her mother cut off even the beginnings of her words, and her father only said, "them." Ann didn't know who "them" was, but she wouldn't be going to school with them. She'd be going to *private* school, across the bridge, with all new kids, all new people.

The Indian River, a ribbon of blue, divided the mainland from the coast, and her new school was there, close to the beach, where the live oaks spread their branches over narrow streets and winding driveways. Past the polo fields and hotels and boutique shops and restaurants, where all the cars were shiny, and everyone's yard looked like the Keene Botanical Gardens, a riot of color and wide-leaf plants. Where everyone had a dark-skinned gardener who spoke Spanish instead of English, and everyone's backyard shimmered with a landlocked in-ground pool. Years later, she'd point out this natural border to Kate: all the rich people lived on the island, everyone who worked for them lived on the mainland.

The kids at the new school had familiar names, names from the backs of pineapple cans, names they shared with politicians on the local news, the names of theme parks and breweries. But they all wore uniforms, so it was hard to tell at first who lived on which side of the Indian River, at least for Ann. But the other girls knew. There were the girls who wore GH Bass & Co. Boat Shoes. And there were the girls who wore J.C. Penney Eastlands. Just a very small green tag separated them, as wide as the river under the four-lane bridge.

As a new student, Ann was paired with Lisa, who walked her between classes and introduced her to the other sixth-grade girls. Each morning Ann brushed her hair smooth into a high ponytail, just like the other girls. She let her socks slip into the backs of her shoes, just like the other girls. She laughed at the English teacher, Mrs. Kayle, behind her back, just like the other girls, because Mrs. Kayle reeked of cigarettes. On the first day of class Mrs. Kayle had been shocked to find out Ann didn't know how to diagram sentences, had never learned at her last school. Laughing at Mrs. Kayle, all six-foot-two of her, all frumpy, below-the-knee skirt and pilling cardigan of her, was a coping mechanism for Ann, caught out in that class as just another public school girl from the other side of the river.

And maybe things would have gone on being fine at this new school, with its manicured gardens and silent brown-skinned gardeners, its annual gala fundraisers, its likely path to the Ivy League or at least a respectable second-tier college, if Ann hadn't misjudged the workings of nascent preteen desire, the complicated dance of crushes and flirtation, the importance of confidences and secrets. Lisa's friends had become her friends, welcoming her to their lunch table in the concrete courtyard, their standing around and talking before and after school in the walkways shadowed with a lattice of creeping banyan and sea grape, overlooking her silences, her fumbling when they asked if she had brothers or sisters.

But when Karen told them she liked Brian and spent weeks talking about his eyes, and how she thought he liked her too, sitting behind her in algebra, always waiting a second too long to take the papers she passed back, lingering as they brushed past each other on their way to band (she played the French horn, he the bassoon), Ann thought she could help. She sat next to Brian in study hall after lunch, and lately he'd been talking to her about some comic book he liked—she'd only half listened, but now thought she'd fish for information, casually bring up Karen. That's what she planned to do, but somehow, she hadn't been subtle, had ended up telling him that Karen liked him. By the end of the day, Lisa, Karen, and the rest of the group were waiting for her by her locker. Karen was red-faced. Lisa looked disappointed, and the other girls gathered like storm clouds behind them, ready to exact revenge.

(Ann had her own secret—his name was P____. She fell in love with him the first day of English class, the day of her humiliation, faced with a board full of slanted lines and blank spaces, a proffered piece of chalk. She knew never to tell the other girls this. So she did know, she must have, that it was wrong to tell Brian about Karen.)

It was never the same again. She would say it was because she lived on the wrong side of the river, or because her shoes were from J.C. Penney. Later, when adolescence hit (and hit), and she felt unhomed in her own skin, she would blame it on other things. Once her parents bought the summer house up north, she'd cling to those summers away, in Wisconsin, with Kate. A place where no one's names were famous, where people didn't pay attention to addresses or boundaries, where no one hired gardeners anyway, where a clean pair of white Keds and pastel socks made her different and interesting, and no one thought about how much they cost.

FIVE

BEFORE ANN

It was a year before Kate would meet Ann. And before Ann there was Mary.

Mary lived with her mother and father in a rental. Kate didn't know anyone who rented a house but didn't own it, so this made Mary special. Between the driveway and the next house was a wooden fence all the way to the narrow backyard, and there was a back porch with no rails where the garbage cans sat, and cardboard boxes, and scraps of carpeting. Mary's mother wore big sunglasses, and her father never wore a shirt. The closet in Mary's bedroom was almost as big as her room and it was filled with stuffed animals and Mary would show them all to Kate, and tell her all their names, even though they were too old to play with stuffed animals. Kate knew they were cheap—prizes from carnival games with the stuffing leaking from seams and eyes that were glued on instead of stitched. They smelled like sawdust and gasoline and made Kate think of the ride boys and fair stalls on the midway at the county fair, the lanky men with crooked teeth spitting into brown bottles that she wasn't supposed to talk to or even look at too long.

"And this one is Brownie, and this one is…" Mary would reach into the pile, grabbing another shabby bear or elephant, "…Margaret, and this one is…" she'd say, pushing the pile farther into the closet, "…Panda." And Kate would listen to the whisper-soliloquy again.

"This one"—Mary's voice would perk up—"…is from Ann." And she'd pull out a nicer plush toy, the fur unmatted, still soft to the touch.

"Who's Ann?"

"Ann's my friend," Mary answered, "but she's in Florida now. She lives in Florida in the winter."

When the girls got too loud, giggling or running up and down the stairs from the first floor living room to Mary's bedroom upstairs, a door would slam, and Mary's father would stomp after them, bare-footed, bare-chested, red-faced. He worked third shift and slept all day, and the girls were supposed to be quiet, but sometimes they forgot. Mary's dad would burst out of the first-floor bedroom, which probably was supposed to be a dining room, in rumpled jeans with his hair stuck to the sides of his face by sleep. His arms were marked with faded blue tattoos across his biceps, and right above the waist of his jeans his stomach cut in on the sides, making a V-shape when he breathed heavy or was angry. Kate thought this was called "wiry," this kind of man-body, this kind of strength, and sometimes when he moved the boxes off the kitchen table or hauled the garbage cans to the front street she noticed how all the veins stood up on his forearms, blue and green under the skin, and she wondered if they would be soft to touch.

A few years later, when Kate's mom moved out, they'd live in this house that had been Mary's. They'd rent too—until her mom was able to buy a house of their own. The scraps of carpeting were gone from the back porch, and there was fresh paint on the walls and over the wide boards of the plank floors, but it was still Mary's house. Kate and Jake would share the room that had been Mary's, and Kate would always think of it as *Mary's Room*, but the closet was mostly empty then. The closet that was always a good space to hide from whatever needed to be hidden from—but by then, even when Kate was scared, she didn't know how to name what she was scared of.

"Damn it, Mary!" her father would yell, climbing the stairs, and behind him would come Mary's mother, padding softly, all hands, trying to soothe him. Once she forgot her sunglasses and Kate saw the one eye, swollen and purple-black, and the other eye where the bruise had faded to yellow and green.

Mary would take Kate's hand and they'd retreat into the closet, into the pile of stuffed animals, and hide and wait to hear the heavy footsteps go back downstairs, the retreating voices. When they extricated themselves from the colored fur and sateen, polystyrene bits clung to their skin and hair, alive with static. And then one day Mary was gone, and when Kate asked the teacher where she was after the third day, her teacher didn't seem to hear her and didn't answer.

• • •

And then Kate met Jaimie. And Jaimie was Ann's doppelganger, but Kate didn't know it. Jaimie had shoulder-length blond hair, blunt-cut bangs. She wore Keds, even in winter, and favored pastels, crew-neck sweaters and straight-leg jeans. She lived on the lake, in one of the summer rentals, but it was winter, and in the winter the rentals were cheap.

Jaimie lived with her dad, but he was never home. Whenever Kate visited her grandparents, she walked over to Jaimie's, and they prank-called boys or listened to the radio, or read *Tigerbeat*, or did anything but talk about school. They spent an entire afternoon trying teal mascara with different combinations of eye shadow, new hair-crimping techniques. They'd lay on Jaimie's bed, laughing and talking.

At Jaimie's, Kate learned what it meant to love: the pleasures of the back of the neck, and sweat, of pressing against each other and breathing with no talking and no eye contact and no admission that anything at all was happening. She learned how fingers and hands can move of their own volition, how legs can scissor and fit together perfectly, and all the places on the body that can press and bend. She learned all the ways skin can smell. She learned that even straight blond hair curled at the base of the neck, underneath. She learned that minutes, then hours, can pass with no word of acknowledgement.

She learned that your best friend can move away without ever telling you she's leaving; that one day, she can just be gone. And since you never talked about it before, now you'll never be able to talk about it.

• • •

Here's how Ann said they met: in the middle school cafeteria, Ann saw a girl who looked like a boy she knew. She walked up to her and said, "Are you Jake's sister?" And that was Kate.

But Kate knows it's because of Mary. Mary said a girl named Ann would be back in the spring. And Mary was Kate's first dangerous friend.

SIX
REAL SISTERS

After Kate's parents split up and Ann's parents split up, they planned to introduce each set of now-single parents to the other. But both of their fathers weren't cooperating. Ann's dad got married right away, and Ann got two new step-sisters, but Ann said they weren't really her step-sisters and that *she* wasn't really her step-mother, *she* was her father's wife, but anyway they ruined that part of the plan. And Kate's dad had a girlfriend right away, then a fiancée, then a wife too. But even after her parents divorced, Ann kept spending summers into September up north at her father's house in Wisconsin, but winters through the end of school in Florida at her mother's, so it didn't seem like much had changed.

It was years before Kate realized that Ann wasn't an only child, not really, that once she hadn't been. All those summers and early falls, Kate had walked past the posed pictures of a little girl and a little boy—the little girl in a ruffled dress with strawberries stitched on, the boy in little boots and shorts—

but somehow hadn't ever thought the little girl was Ann. That little girl had nearly-brown hair, a stiff smile, and didn't look anything like Ann. And maybe it was strange that there was two of everything in the house—two twin beds, two bedside tables, and two versions of every toy, but Kate never noticed enough to ask.

The first time Ann said something about Charlie that Kate heard, she asked, "Who's Charlie?" and Ann answered, quiet and patient, as if she didn't notice that her best friend seemed not to know about her little brother who died. About the little brother she must have talked about before that Kate hadn't heard. They were in the back bedroom, rifling through piles of dirty laundry to find a bathing suit for Kate to borrow, and Ann put a Snoopy plush toy back on the top shelf and said, "That's Charlie's."

"Who's Charlie?"

"Charlie's my brother, he died."

"Oh." And Kate stopped looking for the suit but didn't know what else to say. They were going to go swimming in the pond, probably to play King of the Raft, Kate's favorite game, because she always won, and she loved winning, but even she knew that she should ask a question or maybe say something else, probably the wrong thing: "I didn't know you had a brother."

"Yes, you did, you just forgot," and Ann went back to the pile of laundry.

Kate had two brothers. Jake was littler, and when he was really little she hated him, but now they were close. Since their mom moved out they went back and forth between Mom's house and Dad's house every two days, and while they were living in the first of Mom's houses, they shared a bedroom with bunk beds and spent most nights talking late even after they were supposed to be asleep. Kate remembered that when she read something that scared her—like the rape stories in her mom's magazines—or saw those news stories about the killer a few counties over, she'd crawl into bed with Jake and sleep with him. Even though he was littler, she felt safer sleeping next to him. When he was asleep, he'd roll closer, and pretty soon he'd be wrapped around her, arms and legs crossed, pinioning her, and she'd be able to fall asleep, convinced that somehow she was comforting him.

Her older brother, Robbie, didn't really talk to her anymore. She used to love him more than anything, and one of her favorite stories her parents used to tell her was that she was Robbie's baby. When he first started talking in sentences, he'd asked Santa for a "baby di-da" for Christmas, and that's when they decided they had to have a little girl. But now they didn't tell her stories together anymore, and Robbie wasn't really around. He was older and didn't want to go back and forth with her and Jake so stayed all the time at Dad's house. Kate knew that the way she used to have Robbie as a brother but didn't anymore wasn't the same way Ann used to have Charlie as a brother but didn't anymore. But that's maybe what she wanted to say.

• • •

Charlie had died of cancer when he was really little, only five years old. What Ann remembered most was visiting him in the hospital and seeing lots of doctors and that her parents were always busy driving to doctors and hospitals and driving Ann to see her brother. She felt lonely most of the time, not for her brother, but lonely for her parents. There was one time when she got the flu and threw up all over the kitchen, big gulping sobs of throw-up, and even though she felt terrible she also felt happy because her mom held her hair back when she was in the bathroom later and held a wet washcloth to her forehead, and her dad carried her to bed and tucked her in and read her a story and stayed with her and called her "my baby."

The next time they went to the hospital she had a tantrum right in the lobby, even though she was a big seven-year-old girl, and her mom started crying. Ann started to drop her shoulders when she went through the automatic doors, and by the time they got to the middle of the lobby, right in front of the big desk, she was a puddle of sweater and coat and hat, her shoes trailing off her feet that were wearing mismatched socks.

It was a silent tantrum, all body, all the body's will. The power of language is known to children, to little girls, raised on fairy tales where the protagonist's utterances make things happen. The tantrum in the verbal child is the child resisting this—

this utterance that can make things happen. To not say, "I hate…" or "I wish…" or "I want…" shows strength of will. Even then, Ann knew there were things she couldn't say. Words are spells and curses, they make things happen. So she simply collapsed into the puddle of clothing and tears.

"Goddamn it, Ann!" her father swore, grabbing her hand hard and pulling her to the elevator, but his eyes were starting to turn red too.

"I've got her," her mom said. "You go up." She took Ann into the gift shop and let her pick out a stuffed animal. Ann picked a stuffed Woodstock toy, from the Charlie Brown movies, but then her mom said, "Why don't you pick out one for Charlie?"

And then Ann knew it was a trick—it wasn't really a special treat for her, it was all about Charlie again, so she got him the Snoopy and when they got to his room, she marched up to his bed and set it next to him and then went to sit in the chair by the window and looked out but wouldn't talk to him at all that visit.

Her mom sat on the edge of his bed, playing *Go Fish* on the tray that swiveled over the bed, and her dad played with the TV, looking over at Ann every once in a while, but leaving her alone. Charlie called her name a couple times but she ignored him, pretending to be fascinated by her cuticles, or the pattern of unclaimed parking spots in the lot below. He had tubes in his nose, and a needle and drip in his arm connected to a wheelie-machine, and there were a few other machines that beeped and made burping sounds. But mostly everything seemed very white: white sheets, white blankets and pillows, the white floors and walls that were white too. The curtains on the windows were pulled all the way back, but the midwinter coastal light looked sickly.

• • •

When Charlie was really dying for the last time, Ann's mom disappeared for a few weeks. Ann would hear her dad talking on the phone in whispers, and sometimes yelling, and his eyes were always red. Whenever he went to the hospital, he called a babysitter for Ann. One day when she came home from school, Snoopy was on the top shelf of her closet, next to Woodstock.

Her mom came home a few days later and stayed under the covers in the bed crying for the next week, her suitcase open and still packed on the floor. Her dad slept on the couch when he slept at all, but mostly they both sat at the kitchen table staring at each other. Years later, Ann's father was drunk and blurted it all out: her mom had taken off about two weeks before Charlie died. No one could find her. Her dad's sister finally tracked her down the morning after their baby boy had died—she was in Cincinnati, with *some boyfriend*, taking a *fucking vacation.*

• • •

Kate loved staying at Ann's house. All day long her mom would hang out in the kitchen, and all night they'd sit at the kitchen table, playing cards or talking. Ann's mom would drink from her tumbler of ice and whiskey, and the girls would make their pretend-drinks of Tang and ice, salted with bitters. The first time Ann's parents split up, all Kate could think was that they wouldn't have these nights anymore—Ann's house was the first place she had veal burgers, their silverware looked like gold, and all their glasses were double-walled, so your drinks didn't sweat.

The second time Ann's parents split up, all Kate could think about was *The Plan*. This time it all made sense—Ann's dad and Kate's mom, Kate's dad and Ann's mom. This way they could be sisters, real sisters.

SEVEN
SPINNING

The two not-sisters, almost-sisters, could-be-sisters arrive at the palace, this castle by the sea. Nestled into a cliff, the stairs curve down to the rooms, and the front of the palace is open to the sea air, and more stairs curve down to the rocks and water, but in the months they stay there, neither Ann nor Kate remember ever tripping down to the water to see if there were sirens or sea-monsters hiding in the surf.

Someday Kate will come across the poem that says "I do not they will sing to me," and think of the castle by the sea. Sirens sing to sailors—luring them to their deaths. In stories, the sirens are female, the marks men. And the stories, of course, are told by men—the men who get away, the men who come upon the wreckage of their compatriots lost to the sea, the men who dream of women's voices. *Sing a song of sirens that lure sailors to their deaths.* In that other story, the teller imagines a singer might sacrifice her voice for legs; he can only imagine these two choices: voices or legs. But Kate could not imagine a scenario where she would sacrifice her voice for any promise of future happiness—the beloved, or the legs to find him. And neither Kate nor Ann understand these losses—they have voices and legs and both their hands. Current wisdom suggests that mermaids were only manatees, soft-fleshed, longed for after many months away from female comfort. The girls do not understand metaphor, not yet, but they will.

Ann and Kate are American not-sisters, come to stay in Acapulco, and they bring their American habits. They are unused to stone couches, and hurricane shutters, and workmen repainting the walls a different color every week. They are unused to leaving dishes, the morning bowls ringed with blue milk and soggy flakes, for Lupe, the maid. Everyone in the host family tells them, "Lupe will get it." But they cannot help gathering their used tissues, tidying their own shoes and socks, folding their own laundry, and saying "pleases" and "thank yous" even though every time they do someone looks at them sideways as if they are unable to learn the right things to do and say.

And when they wake in the early morning to their twin beds shuddering side by side on the stone floors, they think *magic*, but the brother says it is only a little earthquake. And when they see lizards skittering over the tops of doorframes and hallways, they try to speak to the green things, remembering the stories read to them as loved children, but these animals do not answer back.

After Ann marries, Kate will visit their small Florida town, and the new husband will drive them from inlet to inlet, small fishing cove to gated canal outlet, playing host, trying to find manatees. He will tell Kate a story of fishing as a child when a manatee approached the boat and he swam with it, bobbing in the waves, floating calmly for minutes that felt like hours, his grandfather laughing from the boat. Later, his grandfather would tell him the manatees approach during mating season, that swimming with humans excites them. Skin is skin, the sun reflects off it bared, whatever species. And if you reached out a hand to touch the smooth-rough shimmering-callused hide, you did not know.

Perhaps those sailors saw the sun glinting off bared skin, and were tricked by the chin. Only a few species have chins—humans and manatees among them. Perhaps they saw the beasts in profile. It's an evolutionary puzzle, the chin. Theories abound: perhaps they are necessary for speech—our voices require extra bone to distribute the stress; perhaps it's some sort of sex selection, developed in perfect synchrony in us all; perhaps it offers some protection against our more violent natures—the chin absorbs a blow, protecting the vulnerable throat. None of these theories are well supported finally. But the theories all circle what we most want to explain, whether in our evolutionary natures or our fairy tales—the mysteries of voice and sex and violence.

• • •

The girls are fourteen—and fourteen is the year for transformation, for hiding away and becoming. Their parents have sent them to the house by the sea for the summer, forgetting the stories. In the fall, they will both go to high school, different schools, where they will be the youngest, and need to navigate the hallways and rooms where stories of voice and sex and violence are woven into Civics and College Prep English like invisible footnotes on the page. But they will only be analyzing the most obvious context and plot; learning subtext will come later. Neither of them have beauty or talent enough to draw anyone's malice—not yet.

Ann is one kind of fourteen. Lately her face has ribboned with acne, bright bursts that shade the sides of her cheeks, where her blond hair falls and half-covers the outbreak; half her suitcase is lotions and creams. After a week, the host-mother takes her aside, gives her a "special" remedy—it is a half-used cylinder, all the text in Spanish. But if they put the gritty paste on a pimple, it dries to white by the next morning when they wake. She gives them the remainder as a parting gift. Back home, they will try to translate the text, discover it is diaper rash cream, this miracle unguent, this savior of teenage faces. For years, Ann will find no better remedy.

And Kate is another kind of fourteen. Her long brown hair curls down her back, curls over her shoulders where the ends frame her chest, nipping under the underwire that lifts and supports. The underwire that slips its casing in the dryer, becomes a projectile, clamoring in the tumble-dry, impaling delicates and soft socks. She knows to walk with her shoulders back—hunching makes her an easier target. She has learned how to sweep her hair off her forehead with one hand, to swing her hips and pretend she doesn't notice anyone noticing how she walks. She only wears two-piece bathing suits here—back home, her father won't allow it. But she hid them in a special section of her suitcase that he didn't know was there. So they both come with their armor: Ann her creams to make her face beautiful; Kate her strips of Spandex and Lycra that detract all attention from her face. Both are convinced someone will be looking.

Auto-reflexivity requires clear signposts, inserted by the author, that reference other texts, but also require reflection, within the text, on the text's intertextual condition: self-conscious references to fairy tales and fairy tale themes and elements, but also references to the references of fairy tales throughout. This should blur the boundaries between genre—here, between the artifice of story and narrator, between the half-hearted pretenses of fictionalized characters that are somehow not the author. The switching between third-person limited omniscient narration and the inclusive second-person. The author must be either Kate or Ann. Which.

The daily Ball, the marriage market, is Plaza Bahia. Most days, the mother drives them into town in the reeking heat, past piles of garbage gathered loosely in the street, past the stooped haunches of unhomed dogs rifling through it. The car drives down from the hills, and they watch from the back-seat as the scenery changes from the houses with their wrought-metal gates and courtyards to taller buildings and narrow sidewalks. To chipped cement and stucco in ice-cream colors, rebar exposed. In the center of town, the buses and taxis congregate, and she drops them off in front of the mall amidst the blue smoke and the smells of exhaust and burnt meat, rotting produce. She'll be back in the afternoon, and they have the day to wander the shops, wander the beach, wander the town with their pidgin Spanish, shop and haggle.

At the entrance to Plaza Bahia, they buy shave ice and practice their vocabulary, ordering combinations of fruits, rolling their *r*'s, practicing their accents. On the beach, they eat mangos on sticks, tamarind, hollowed coconuts. Boys offer them beers from coolers. Their chaperone brother is always there to frown or send them off. Their chaperone sister is only twelve; she doesn't know the danger of fourteen, the need to hide away. The danger of hiding away.

If they want to swim, they go to Boca Chica, the hotel with the stone steps into the water, where they can open their eyes and see the bright little fishes, the dream of landlocked girls. The salt stings at first, but the fish are cobalt and yellow, or zebra-striped, and they can pretend they are on a TV documentary, swimming the reefs, letting their hair ride the undersea currents as they gesture under the water to each other, speak in signs, their special language. Or they sneak into the fancy hotels and pretend they are guests. If you walk a certain way and claim a striped beach cabana like you own it, no one questions you. The sand is gray-white, and the beach slopes so gradually that they can be hundreds of yards from shore before the water touches their bathing suit bottoms. "Watch for fins," the brother says. "There are sharks here."

Men-of-war glitter like deflated balloons, iridescent, incandescent. *Do not touch the trembling thing.* This is a warning. Things that are beautiful can also be dangerous. Things that are beautiful are often dangerous. Tell this to Kate when she wears the white bikini with the dangling gold coins and pretends to belong at the bar. Tell this to Ann when she stares open-mouthed at the beautiful boy who whistles at the traffic light. Underwater, a lionfish sways in the current.

But they do not swim in the bay, where what looks like a jellyfish at first is really just a plastic bag, caught up in the green water, riding the current with other refuse. It fills and empties as the waves make their concentric circular movements, ending in sand. "We don't swim in the bay," the sister tells them. Down the beach, everyone else is splashing and running in the surf, but the breakers roil with trash: bags and pop tops, discarded Band-Aids, and unidentifiable pieces of paper and plastic. This beach is for walking only—be careful about eye contact, smiling too long, don't talk to the people hawking hair braiding, cheap trinkets, souvenir T-shirts, and especially the boys. "Danger is everywhere," the father warns them, especially for fourteen-year-old girls.

• • •

There are things you will not be able to tell your mother, even in the cool of the basement, even when she is distracted by the hissing of the iron, the percussive shake of the spray starch. The pile of rumpled, button-down men's shirts waits, and you try to tell her. Things have happened and you need help. You end up covering your face with a pillowcase, which she will iron once she's done with the pile of your father's shirts, if she is the kind of mother that still irons your father's shirts.

You will tell her: once something happened with the neighbor boy, and you did not understand it, but now you do.

You will tell her: once something happened when you were away, and you did not understand it at the time, but now you do.

You will tell her: skin and touch feels good. But you did not know desire until you learned shame—they must go hand in hand. That is the first lesson. And you have learned shame. And now you are done for.

You will tell her: things happened and now you understand and now you need her help but you do not know how to ask. You have unlearned how to speak—having swallowed fear and anger, worried what utterance can do.

• • •

There are Princes, and False-Princes, and Clever Hanses. If he is a true Prince, the parents will acquiesce, and no brother-chaperone is required. A true Prince drives his own big car, or has a driver. A true Prince has a castle even more impressive than this—his iron-gated home has no need for glass-shard fences set into wet concrete. The bougainvillea is always lush, the blossoms uncrushed. When he and Kate walk through these overgrown paths, she sees the gardener and realizes this unkemptness is aesthetic, not haphazard. She thinks the rich are funny, the way they cultivate the overgrown vines, the chinked stonework and rangy blooms. The true Prince visits at the house enough times to make the family feel safe—he is a true Prince. And she is just an American girl, one who wears her shorts too short and is unimpressed with his name and who his father is. If she isn't wise enough to know, why would they tell her?

Clever Hans isn't really clever, but he's also no Prince. Lucky Hans isn't really lucky, but he thinks he is. When Hans calls, he calls for Ann. And the mother and father don't even need to ask his name—they know he is no Prince. Somehow they can see, with magical vision, that even though his skin is smooth, it's more mestizo than Spanish; that even though he's kind and well-spoken, his hands are already rough from the work he'll be doing for the rest of his life. They cannot be fooled. So when he wants to see Ann, they agree, but it must be during the day and the brother-chaperone, sister-chaperone, and Kate must go too—there's safety in this group that troops downtown where likely Hans lives with his mother and brothers and sisters, and come nightfall the girls will be safe at home behind the walls of their palace where the moonlight glitters on glass-shard fences.

But Hans brings a friend for Kate—and "yes," he says, "he's *guapo*," but Kate doesn't agree, so when Ann and Hans walk down the beach, awkwardly stumbling in the sand, she doesn't go along. Chaperone-brother is there, ready to perform his duty. Kate stares at the friend, at the fly that lands on the corner of his mouth, that somehow he doesn't seem to notice, and she doesn't even try to speak to him in her pidgin Spanish, and after a while he gives up too. Ann knows it will not work—despite Hans's shy smile, the kindness of his hand as he offers it to her to help her up the stairs from the beach. If Kate will not assist with the romance, there is no hope for a happy ending.

The Prince takes Kate out for dinner, but always to the same place, and she always orders the same thing. Each time they go, she takes a matchbook souvenir, and these fill the secret compartment in her suitcase, ready for the trip home. He insists on opening her car door everywhere, and she pretends to be irritated by it until she is truly irritated by it—how she must sit and wait in her seat for him to let her out. When she tries to let herself out, it is as if there is a child lock even on the front passenger door, and she is trapped, immobilized. He explains that it is respectful to open the door for a lady, it is how he was raised. She must wait for him. To try to open the door herself embarrasses him—the valet thinks he isn't a gentleman. She tries to explain that women can do things for themselves, that she isn't a child, that she isn't that kind of girl. But he disapproves of her argument; he is a True Prince.

And of course he is very handsome. Only one picture of him will survive, but she will be taken aback, again and again, by how very handsome he is.

In the story, the girl is revealed to be a true princess because someone sees her. Although she may not know how to talk to the maid, or that good girls don't dress that way, or that she shouldn't be pulling at the handle of the car door, shoving the weight of her shoulder against the upholstery, she is a true princess when she cannot sleep for the pebble wedged under twenty mattresses and twenty featherbeds. The only pebbles that will bother Kate will be the ones on the beach, the private beach near the Navy station, where there is no one around to yell to anyway. And that word is the same in English and Spanish, so he shouldn't pretend he didn't understand.

In the story, the Prince's mother recognizes the true Princess, despite her rain-wet clothes, her muddy shoes, her bedraggledness. But she never met his mother.

. . .

At the skate rink, they have gone—all the children—for a day of being children. The brother and sister lace up their skates. The littlest sister grasps her mother's hand. Ann and Kate hold hands, racing around the outdoor cement track, laughing like the children they've always been—before this summer. Ann's legs are long and getting longer—she's shooting up. Never again will she and Kate be able to wear any of the same clothes. Kate is done growing—never again will she get any taller or be any more beautiful. Fourteen is the beginning for Ann; for Kate it's the end.

Each day this summer, they've been different people. One day Ann will be painting on the terrace with the littlest sister and ignore Kate when she comes in from seeing the Prince. One day they'll be swimming in the pool, pretending to be dolphins, both showing off for the workmen next door. One day Kate will be getting ready to go out and Ann will have hidden the brother under the bed; his laughter gives him away. One day Ann will hide all Kate's underwear, thinking that might keep her home. In the shoebox of photographs, there are pictures of them all, crouched into the tiled shower, washing the chlorine from their suits, long hair whipping faces, smiles caught in the light filtered through the glass block.

At the skate rink, they are building new ramps adjacent, and the neighborhood boys are waiting, impatient, for the new half-pipe, the stairsets, the funboxes. It is the end of one thing and the beginning of another. At the skate rink, all the concrete has yellowed and spalled. The wide oval is deserted, except for the children being children, maybe for the last time.

At the skate rink, the False-Prince lured her away. He plied her with compliments. She is dumb as Snow White, tricked for a stay-lace and a comb. What Kate most wants is to be done with fourteen. By the time he's led her, Bambi-legged in the heavy skates, beyond the half wall, out of sight of the mother, she sees his friends. The False-Prince is beautiful—caramel hair that curls and touches his shoulders, mirrored glasses so she cannot see his eyes. His friends don't bother to hide their eyes.

As the False-Prince reaches for her, she finally hears him, "Do you work?" and knows that he is the False-Prince. She looks across the cement divider but cannot see Ann.

But she looks. Of course she does. The girl in the tale always looks, and the looking brings good or ill. This time, she sees the pile of bodies, the limbs caught up where they fell, the four of them: Ann, the brother, the sister, and the littlest sister. They are laughing like children, their legs in the air.

He says again, "Do you work?" And she realizes that he's speaking English.

The legs in the air swing and jerk. The heavy skates roll at the ends of the legs, the wheels spinning.

EIGHT
WILL

The tales teach obedience and submission. The tales teach disobedience and deceit. The tales are ambiguous. The tales teach female competition—mothers and daughters, sisters and wives.

The Princess refuses to hide away—she hears of sharp points and soft flesh, and she knows what that means. She is shown rooms of flax and linen, uncarded wool, drop spindles and machines one works with one's feet. She closes the doors softly and returns to the large halls that open into other halls that open into hallways where the front doors swing wide to open lawns and beyond the lawns fields that stretch beyond the horizon into the world.

And when her father tells her to be careful she smiles. And when her mother takes her hand and tells her to be careful she smiles. And when her new friend invites her to visit the next kingdom, to meet some princes, she smiles.

Her prince is named Will, and her friend says he is handsome and kind. The other prince is named

Nick and he is newly freed from an entanglement with another, who turned ogre. They are sneaking to the next kingdom, and over the lengthy ride they rehash the ways of women: the carping and back-stabbing, the jealousies and ordinary unkindnesses. The little hills rise between quarries and sandpits, the stepped cut-away hills sometimes blocking the late afternoon sun as it sets. When they crest one hill, the friend crosses her fingers, whispers, "please don't pick me up, please don't pick me up," and the Princess is surprised until she sees the flash of red and blue lights in the back window and knows they have been driving too fast, racing to the princes awaiting them.

They go for dinner, and Will's dark hair catch-es the soft light of candle and stoop-light. His hand touches the lower part of her back. He is tall and older, heading to college in the fall. She is fifteen and knows a thing or two about princes.

After dinner, her friend and Nick need some time alone, so she and Will drive around, through the de-serted streets of this small Midwestern town, back and forth on the main drive quiet on a Wednesday night. At home, her homework is neatly done, folded and stapled, waiting for tomorrow. There is no prac-tice on Wednesday nights, the one night reserved for church classes. He pulls into the empty lot behind the false fronts of small-town downtown stores; the few cars passing through are blocked from view. The inlet and outlet to the lot are blocked from view by dumpsters filled with flattened cardboard boxes.

And Will reveals his naming—all hands. There is a tape in the tape player that plays one song and one song only, on constant repeat.

She is thankful for her too-tight jeans, difficult to force off. For the gearshift in the middle he has trouble maneuvering around. For elbows and knees and the way she can curl herself into a ball and fit down into the wheel well where he cannot force or cajole her out. For the nails she lets grow long. Only when she scratches his face and draws blood, leaves a mark, does he give up.

There is a tape in the tape player that plays one song and one song only, on constant repeat. She counts eight times the song cycles through.

"Jesus fucking Christ," he says, putting the car in gear. They drive back to Nick's house.

Inside the door, she bangs on the bathroom door, barges in. Her friend is pushed up against the bathroom vanity, but smiling.

"Let's go," the Princess says.

"In a minute…" and Nick looks at her angrily over his shoulder.

"No, now," and then she waits for what seems like another eight cycles of the song in the kitchen, across the room from Will, until the bathroom door opens and they emerge, smoothing down their clothes, buttoning things.

In the car on the way home, cresting the hills, the Princess tells her friend about Will. About what almost happened. About how hard she had to fight.

"Oh, yeah," her friend says, "he can be kind of pushy..."

The Princess's mouth hangs open in the dark and silent car.

"We used to go out. He tried that with me—it's easier just to give in." No sound comes out of the Princess's mouth. She curls into the bucket seat, nearly as small as she curled into the wheel well, but no one is trying to force her legs apart, to stick his tongue into her mouth. "You didn't have to make such a big deal out of it," her friend says.

• • •

It is the next year, and the Princess actually looks like a princess, dressed in a ball gown and glittering. She is layered in velvet, cut glass jeweled at her neck. Someone taps her shoulder, and there is Will.

"Hi," he says, and he is holding her former friend's hand. "You look really beautiful." He is holding her former friend's hand, and they walk away into the night. Nothing has happened. Nothing has happened. Nothing happened.

• • •

Who ordered the harvest of your heart? Who broke the worst curse and taught you that false death— the utterly passive body—was the way to win a prince? Who directed you to trim your own heel, its fat curve of flesh, and proffered the blade, handle-first, as an offer of kindness?

• • •

There is this business of names—as if they signify, as if they mean, as if they are a coming true, a hid-

den wish, a talent to be revealed or a secret guard-
ed. Something one must become.

His name was something biblical. Or something
Viking.

There were each other's salvation. Or each other's albatrosses.

The Princess set off on a long journey, with many
tests along the way. The first was to escape.

She'd met him-of-the-biblical-name when she
was with her first high school boyfriend, who shall
remain nameless here, hardly worth the nanocents
of the nanoseconds the inkjet would take to commit
it to consumer-recycled paper. But he introduced her
to the second high school boyfriend, who showed
her what kindness was, and that touch could be
insistent yet shy, something searching, something
they could discover together. Even then, she knew
it would end in tragedy. She has a picture from that
year, and she thought she looked pretty, her hair
blunt cut, bobbed at the jawline, and the ill-timed
flash didn't make her eyes red like some ogre finding daylight after too long in a cave, but rather like
some girl who might have magic after all. The picture survives; that moment is immortalized.

They planned—in the way of the young—to base
a life on that moment, the camera's flash catching
them quick. She applied to school nearby, to wait
another year for him to finish high school, and then
they would move away together—from this Kingdom that never fit them. Where they found each other because neither of them found a place anywhere

else. The Princess submitted her application, paid her deposit, readied her boxes and brain, and he-of-the-biblical-name told her in July he didn't love her anymore. Nothing more than that. That was that. And that was the first test.

Maybe they were each other's beards.

When she finally asked him, he said, "No, of course not," and that was a kindness. Months later, when he said, "Yes, I think so," that was also a kindness. He was trying not to hurt her. But either way, all she felt was loss.

• • •

If you are a certain kind of Princess, a princess in hiding, more sackcloth than glitter, you have this story. No Prince asks if you will try the shoe—there is no one proffering a blade, offering you the option to peel the fat of your heel. You and he are drawn to each other—and you explore the quiet spaces of back seats and rooms when parents aren't home. You know the long silences of phone calls when you are late, when the condom slips, when you both feel trapped by something else. But because kindness is your first language of love, you survive. For that, you will always be grateful. And for learning what loss is. Because whether he is or isn't, it is irrevocable— you are not what he wants. The oven clock ticks too loudly, and you sob in the kitchen, and when your mother asks you what is wrong, there is no way to tell her: there is no truth you can tell.

• • •

She escaped anyway. Shorn that cute bob hair, dyed it purple-black, dressed only in jeans and long-sleeve tees, the cuffs of everything too long, her boots heavy-soled. Heavy souled. No Princess now.

Escape is not only geographic—the boundaries of kingdoms and townships and flight patterns. Escape is kinship and inheritance and the twin that you carry. Even in these different hills, the purple-haired Not-Princess could not be far enough away from he-of-the-biblical-name.

• • •

Later, this first loss would be the loss that she would compare all other losses of her adult life with. The losses of childhood are different—they are carried partially by others. They are stitched into the skin of parents, of grandparents, known by the patterns on the wall that was the wall that backgrounded that loss. This loss was wholly her own: hers to carry, or not; hers to pack and take with her; hers to water and feed to be less alone.

• • •

Names can be a coming true. And if there were times she made herself small enough to not be seen and not be hurt, there were times when that smallness became offense rather than defense. When her unwillingness to be reached became iron and provided a way out—a way out across the country and away. And she packed her loss—it slept in the backseat at a few truck stops when she was low on cash. When she lived in Utah for a while, it briefly considered conversion but was unsure how it would handle the temple garments. The Princess must become Will, although it was not what she was named.

NINE
THE PROBLEM WITH KATE

Standing on the street and looking up at the building, it looks like a tower—all height and desire, unrequitable. Only four or five floors tall, but where the stairwell is, there's only a window at the very top. When someone rings the buzzer, usually a boy, either Kate or the flatmate will crane their heads out the top window, and the wind will catch her hair. Kate's hair is newly shorn, and she feels for the first time unlovely—like a twelve-year-old boy. If the boy is someone they know (usually someone Kate knows) they will buzz him in. Because this tower has a door. Because desire is only useful if there's a chance of scaling the wall, of climbing the stairs. Because the only trial required of this suitor is five flights of stairs and the will to climb them—princes are few and far between.

From the top window, they can look to the right, over the river, where the riverboat tourist cruises with jazz bands float, and at night the twinkle lights reflect off the water. To the left is a couple of pedestrian streets and a traffic circle by the pub that stays open until two a.m. At two a.m. it's just a stumble home, hardly dangerous. Farther on is the square and the abbey, and the big covered pedestrian mall where they can buy produce and fresh bread, and farther north along the river is a covered bridge lined by shops and bistros and below the covered bridge is a weir where the water falls over manmade ledges and the trash collects in the corners of the curved steps. And the weir is shallow and the water dirty, hardly beautiful, except at night, after the stumble-home.

The flat was two bedrooms, a kitchen, a long hallway, and a bathroom. One bedroom was smaller but completely surrounded by windows. The other was meant for two girls, two twin beds side by side, but only one small window. Kate gave up the windows for the larger room, pushed the two beds together and bought larger sheets. That flatmate, Deirdre, should have known this was significant.

Even though English is English, "flatmate" is one of the first things Kate learned to say. Also, what "bird" meant. And the difference between "fanny" in American and British. So the first time a boy says, "swing your fanny up here," you are not taken aback.

Before Deirdre started living with Kate, she'd been a good girl. Her eyes were big at every new thing: learning to look the other way before crossing the street, drinking underage, British boys who were cute until they smiled. Kate knew to hide her big eyes, how to order a drink, how to insult a boy so he didn't know you thought he was cute. At night, over tea in the cramped kitchen, they'd talk about their small towns, their parents who worried about them, how excited they were for the semester living so far from home. Kate spent the first few weeks going out, but she'd always stay out later by herself, and sometimes she'd bring a boy home, and sometimes she'd stumble home alone. Deirdre would throw her shoes at the wall if they got too loud—it was always the talking that was too loud, not the. After, Kate and whoever-the-boy-was would lie awake laughing and talking and from the other side of the wall it sounded so joyful, so carefree, so careless.

One day Deirdre came home and Kate was in the kitchen, using the dull little paring knife to pull the skins off some strange-looking roots. She'd hold the tubers perpendicular to the counter, slip the knife's blade under the dull-colored outer covering and peel it, where it would come off in a strip, unless it hit a knob or joint.

"What are those?" she asked, gesturing to the table.

"They're called *Jerusalem Artichokes*," Kate said. "I found them at the market."

"Oh." She hesitated. "But, but what *are* they?" Deirdre picked one up, and it was heavy and hard in her hand. She sniffed it but didn't smell anything but dirt. Kate laughed.

"I don't know. I asked the woman selling them, and she said they're a root vegetable, like a potato—

or 'celeraic'—but I don't know what that is either." Kate shrugged.

"What are you going to do with them?" she asked, wrinkling her nose. Kate was the apartment cook, and most of what she made was good, but sometimes her willingness to try new things backfired. On those nights, she and Kate would go get a pub meal and leave the inedible food until morning to clean up—the plates to scrape and wash and put away. But then the "quick dinner" would inevitably turn into something else.

"I'm going to pretend they're potatoes—boil them and mash them…we'll see what it tastes like…" Kate sounded excited, like she always did.

"What's that?" Deirdre asked, pointing at the refrigerator.

"That," Kate answered, and she was really smiling now, "is The Map."

By mid-October, The Map was marked with stars (for each new location) and codes (for what exactly happened) and scores (to track pleasure) to memorialize their semester abroad. Most of The Map was coded for Kate, but her flatmate started to catch up.

A week after The Map had come to be, Kate's best friend, Ann, visited on her own fall break, stayed in the flat, and she and Ann and the Deirdre all went out. One night, at the Firkin, Kate found her mark and Ann found another. They met up the next day around noon. Somehow Ann found her way back, in this foreign city, this layout of streets she didn't know. When the story comes up years later,

Ann will say, "Natalie Holloway." Kate will laugh and say, "Shut the fuck up."

• • •

Late October Deirdre went to a basement office, where everyone was so kind. The lights were muted, and there were secondhand patterned couches, and they offered her a free test. She hadn't been able to eat breakfast for a while, the smell of eggs sending her to the bathroom. After the test came back positive, the counselor sat down with her to discuss her options. She congratulated her and told her how her baby was growing. She told her stories about her children, her own pregnancies, how fulfilled she'd felt to know that she was carrying a baby, carrying new life. Her voice sounded like a 45 played at 78 rpms. Deirdre took her card, the stack of brochures and papers, and left.

When she got home, Kate was making salsa.

"Look at these funny little peppers I found," she yelled when she heard the door open. She held them up as Deirdre came into the kitchen. They were orange and wrinkled, small enough to fit in the palm of a hand.

"What are they?"

"I don't know," Kate said. "I've never seen them before."

"Are they hot?"

"Beats me. I'm going to put a bunch in the salsa. We'll find out…" She looked down at the paper bag full of papers and brochures. "What you got there?"

"Nothing," she said. "What's for dinner?"

• • •

She had the abortion in late November, and Kate took her to the hospital, waited during the procedure, and stuffed the fridge with all her favorite foods—ice cream and croissants and made-ahead pre-portioned pasta with cream sauce and soups cooked down all day. When Dierdre saw the fridge, she said, "It's not my birthday, Kate. I had an abortion."

• • •

Beyond the stone wall is a garden. Blue stone and tall. The walled garden is rows and rows of green leaves, dew-fresh, curled fringes of yet-unknown, yet-untasted. She stares out the window at the cool green, knowing that if she does not get a taste she will die. This is the way of cravings. Years later, the junior year study-abroad flatmate wrote a letter. She said, "What appalls me about you, Kate, is your bravado." Kate saved the letter, slipped it into the junior year study-abroad scrapbook, right next to The Map.

When the semester came to a close and it was time to say good-bye to Deirdre and the girls downstairs, they'd planned an all-night night of food and movies and remembering the semester. Kate made plans with her that-week boyfriend, someone else's husband, and spent the night at his house. He was making dinner, vegetarian risotto with homemade stock, and he put Kate to work, chopping green beans into one-inch lengths. She'd never had risotto before, didn't know about stirring in sharp cheeses, about adding stock slowly to layer flavors. They'd stopped their mise en place for an interlude on the kitchen counter.

She'd brought big portobello mushroom caps and planned to stuff them with cheese. When he saw the cheese, Stilton, he wrinkled his nose.

"Why'd you get Stilton?"

"Why not? What's wrong with Stilton?" Kate didn't know what Stilton was, what it tasted like. At the cheese stall, there'd been a line of people, so she hadn't taken the time to ask for a sample or ask the woman to describe the cheese or how to use it.

"It's too strong—it'll overpower the mushrooms." She looked at him down her nose, something that wasn't easy to do, as he was so much taller, and he was standing so close, towering over her in the small kitchen, his forehead nearly hitting the pots hanging from the rack suspended over the butcher block island.

"Never mind," he said. "Make it how you want. It was just a suggestion…"

"Well, what would you use Stilton for?" Kate asked, remembering that she didn't know him that well, that there was no reason to be getting upset about cooking, about recipes, about a cheese she'd never even heard of before today, an English cheese anyway.

"Stilton would be good in a risotto," he said. But he was making the risotto, and she had brought the things for stuffed mushrooms. But he was right, the cheese was too strong and the mushrooms weren't very good.

After they'd eaten, they'd opened the kitchen door to the back patio so Kate could smoke, and watched a cat slink away in the rain. He made a joke about a snuff film. When she went upstairs, he'd lit candles all over and drawn a hot bath. But the sex made up for that. They spent the morning vacuuming and changing the sheets, removing all evidence of Kate from the house—his wife was coming home that afternoon, and he'd learned from past experience how an errant hair could give him away.

All this time the girls were leaving, their flights spiderwebbing from Heathrow to New York and Chicago and Toronto. Then to smaller regional hubs, then to warm parents' cars waiting to welcome them home. Kate had cancelled her flights, planned to stay the winter holidays with some friends in Blackburn, spend January in London.

When she returned to the flat, everyone was gone. This was how Kate liked to say good-bye: once everyone was gone, to walk through the empty rooms and start missing everyone when she was already missing them. Whenever she left somewhere, she loved the long last look out the back of the car window, the silence apart from any good-byes or hugs. She loved leaving places for the last time. She'd turn around and stare out the curved glass until the known trees, the rooftops, the last line of billboards disappeared over the horizon. But this only worked if she wasn't driving, this only worked if she was leaving by car, leaving some place with trees and houses and billboards. This was Kate's idea of leaving: something a child does, nothing she ever has to manage herself.

• • •

But mostly Kate and Ann will have stories to laugh about. How Kate hooked up with the postman. If you're going to have a one-night stand, don't have it with the postman—you'll see him every day. He and Kate were going at it in the bedroom, and Ann needed something, forgot, and opened the door, saw more of Kate than she needed to see. "In a minute, Ann…" and Kate just kept going. When Kate was busy, she wouldn't stop for anything, not even Ann. That movie had just come out, about Neruda, and even now, they'll joke about *Il Postino* and both roll on the floor laughing.

When the junior year study-abroad stories get going, Ann will say to Kate, "Amanda Knox." But nothing bad has ever happened to Kate.

TEN

THE LOST YEARS

After college, Ann and Kate lost each other for a while. They strayed from The Plan—and once they returned, all the breadcrumbs had been eaten, all the shiny pebbles scattered. Ann took her business degree and headed west: Colorado, and Utah, and Oregon, working at design firms and furniture shops. She had a talent for managing numbers—invoices and bills—but also people, getting the builders and owners and clients to all agree to deadlines and specs. Once she spent a summer making Auto-CAD designs long-distance for a family of Amish builders, their furniture and built-ins highly desired by certain homeowners who thought their unkempt beards, their month-long smell, a certain kind of cachet. They favored rough-cut boards, bedsteads dependent on the circumference of the trees' caliper.

Along the way, she met Mark. By the time Kate finished college, Ann and Mark were living together, buying their own furniture, and no one likes an interloper. When Ann called to say she was leaving

Mark, Kate was free and ready to join her—but Ann hadn't left any gap. She was leaving Mark for Albert.

There is a moment that can't be definitively described. Maybe he had "pushed" her, maybe she had "walked into" him. Either way, she ended up sitting on the bed, surprised by the sudden violence of hands, thinking, *Is this the beginning of something? Or is this the end?* It was always good to have an exit strategy. For a good exit strategy you need: your own bank account, a job that pays, no pets in common, and reliable birth control. Or someone new waiting in the wings. The Someone-New-Waiting-In-The-Wings takes care of most elements missing from the exit strategy, except the pet issue. If you move on to the Someone-New-Waiting-In-The-Wings, don't bring the dog from the last relationship. Trust me.

Kate killed a few years bartending, parlaying her attractive-enough / nonthreatening appearance into good tips. She'd grown up in bars, watched the way her father treated the dispensers of beer and "white ones," watched the way he and his friends shook dice, flirted with the younger women behind the buffer of the bar.

Here's what Kate learned in bars: Always buy the fourth drink. If it's not a policy of the establishment, sneak it. If the establishment counts drinks or keeps careful count of pours, buy it yourself, ringing the free drink conspicuously.

Always overpour, sloppily, in front of the patron.

If you finish a bottle, tell the patron it's free. If it isn't really, make it so.

Flirt with the beta males. Especially the shy ones, who won't make eye contact.

Flirt with the old men. Pretend to believe them when they tell you you remind them of their daughter, their granddaughter, their niece. When they get sloppy later and talk to you like they would never talk to their daughter, their granddaughter, their niece—take it in stride.

When they get sad and want to talk about their wife who died, or left them, or doesn't listen, or doesn't touch them, listen like you've never heard this story before.

Make friends with the wives, the girlfriends. Talk to them like all their beloved has done is talk about them. Listen with full eye contact—don't ever let your eyes slide to the side. They'll never know you're dangerous.

Shake dice and lose. House pays. Create obligation.

Drive the regulars home yourself. Endure their sloppy passes. (One time, you'll get stuck in his drive, the beginning of a blizzard. Put him to bed in his clothes and unlace his boots. Pretend to not be bothered by his Doberman growling at you in the morning on the couch. Accept the sheepish omelet, the shy gift of bacon.) Create obligation.

Challenge the regular who thinks his money buys him whatever he wants. Bide your time—he'll need your help at some point. Every time you see him with his wife, all you'll need to do is catch his eye. Men like this are bankers, mortgage brokers, mayors or representatives in your small town. Create obligation.

She made good tips. One week it was Simon, one of the old-timer regulars, but it was a slow Tuesday, and no one else was in. She listened for hours, holding his hand, where he couldn't see her impatient feet tapping below the bar. By close, his whiskey and ice was all water. Simon always tipped a dime, a quarter if he liked you, but the other bartenders rolled their eyes at him, and he saw everything. Kate never rolled her eyes, and that night he left her a crisp fifty-dollar bill.

And she handled the weddings, casual affairs on the back brick patio, beside the small creek, under the dappled shade of trees. Her coworkers hated working weddings—the gratuity was included in the price, and with the open bar, most people didn't add any bills to the jar on the makeshift table—even with the little sign that said "Tips Appreciated!" that was all curlicues and smiles. They also hated the uniform of black pants and cheap clip-on bowtie. But Kate knew there was still money to be made. Weddings were the best place to be mercenary. Make friends with the bride first, then her wedding party.

When the groom asked for help, she took the tip jar and slung it into the cooler with the chilled white wines and followed him to the men's bathroom, where she found the bride's little sister, underage, in tears, with the best man. She guided her through the back basement to the door that opened to the front street, supporting her in her strappy shoes, all legs, coltish, her skin pale and bluing. She put her in a cab and told her to go home, take a shower, take a nap. She then helped the groom and the best man, revived with a dunk in the ice bucket, get back to the party. And because this was a Wisconsin wedding, the DJ was queuing up the requisite polka tunes.

"Thanks," the new husband said, looking into her eyes a little too long—slinging a meaningful look at his wife across the patio.

"Sure thing," Kate said, and later when the bride asked where her little sister was, Kate said that she hadn't been feeling well, that maybe she'd had a few too many mimosas, and smiled.

Two weeks later her boss called her in, handed her an envelope, already opened.

"This came today," he said, his lips set in a grim line. "You wanna explain it?" Kate looked down at the check addressed to her, signed by the groom, and the memo line that said, "best bartender ever."

"I told you I was a really good bartender," she answered, her own mouth set in its own grim line, but the edges suggesting something of a smile.

"Yup, you did say that. I just want to make clear..." he continued, looking at the stacked boxes of wine, of beer, of Southern Comfort and rail liquor and mixers behind him, "we're only selling drinks here."

It's all creating obligation and cashing in. It's another kind of education. She met Jason in a bar. And then Ann was getting married.

ELEVEN

THE TAXONOMY

Somehow Kate settled down first, but when she says it, she says "settled" and waits a beat too long, in case anyone has missed her meaning. Both she and Ann ended up with the same guy, the Funny Guy. Underlying the jokes and impressions that were a little off was a sweetness not quite hidden.

The tales only present two models for marriage: *Beauty and the Beast* or *Bluebeard*. Love either cures or blinds. But mostly marriage requires negotiation—and the negotiation is with yourself. What you're willing to watch yourself doing—what you're willing to admit to watching yourself doing. Especially the time lapse between jokes-that-hide-pain to anger-that-hides-pain—whether you'll negotiate this if it's inwardly directed, or outwardly directed, or both. Whether you can tell the difference. Maybe you'll have a daughter—and you won't want her to see you negotiating this, won't want her to think that a woman should negotiate this—should know how. Maybe you'll have another self, and that other self will be named Kate, or Ann, and you'll be conscious of what this other self would say. If this is a love story, it's the story of Ann and Kate.

Both Ann and Kate ended up with the Funny Guy who is also the Angry Guy. This is always the problem with the Funny Guy—he must be funny for a reason. Ann's husband, Greg, was only ever the Funny Guy to Kate. By the time Kate knew that something wasn't right between them, it was all over. It's a strange thing to watch a marriage end, to witness it there in front of you, on the weekend you happen to be visiting. Time is slow, and the baby is sleeping, and your flight is leaving in the morning, but no one else can sleep. The guest room is the living room couch, and since the fight isn't over—will never be over now—no one leaves the living room so there's no lying down for Kate, no falling to sleep.

Now that the secret is out, there's no reason to stop talking. Greg will walk in and out, but the little world has closed again, and it's Ann and Kate, heads bent together, rehashing everything they haven't said these last years, every moment of doubt planted and fertilized, until the sprout. And then the smothering, but the seed is hardy. It survives, and you might as well tell the whole story now.

What Kate remembered is that when Ann and Greg got married they eloped, and that would have been the only wedding she'd actually want to be in—Ann the only person she loved enough to walk down the aisle with.

What Kate remembered is that before Luna was born she was scared of Ann's body, always kept a buffer zone, lest she accidentally touch skin, or graze the bump of navel poking out, the nipples that seemed sharp and insistent. Finally, at the airport drop-off, she worked up the courage to touch the belly, briefly, and congratulated herself all the way home.

What Kate remembered is holding Luna in the sling, two months old, carrying her around everywhere, and thinking that this might be as close as she got to loving a baby. Luna, blue-eyed and beautiful, even then—not like those creepy big-headed babies she saw everywhere. Which she said too loudly, at the grocery store, and Greg dropped a container of orange juice before looking around and laughing too hard. They backed slowly away from the spilled sticky orange.

What Kate will remember is Ann saying now, "I don't think he loves me—I don't think he ever loved me," and Kate thinking *How can you be so blind?* This love may not be what you want, and this marriage may be unsalvageable, but to pretend that those are the same thing is a self-deception worthy of only someone like Kate. Ann knows better.

• • •

Kate remembers a fight with Jason, early on, and he said casually that maybe she should stay out of it—that Ann's life wasn't her business. "Don't interfere with my primary relationship," she responded. She tells Ann this story that weekend, and they both laugh—remember The Plan when they were younger, to somehow salvage their desires from their parents' divorces and reconstitute their family the way they wanted. And here they are, sitting in plastic lawn chairs on the St. Augustine grass, as the sun comes up from behind the palmetto, Kate with her coffee, Ann her Diet Coke, sneaking one last cigarette before they head to the airport. Kate is going back to her life, Jason, and Ann will be starting over again.

Kate jokes about "settling down," about "settling," but technically she's not married, and won't be. She and Jason don't have children, and won't. Somehow, Kate hopes this makes them somewhat different—that maybe she hasn't ended up as her mother, setting the table and waiting to see how many places will be claimed, piling through a stack of button-down shirts, the iron and spray starch at the ready. She does do the trick with turning the shirts inside out, avoiding the click click click of the iron against the buttons, but they are her shirts. Jason doesn't work the kind of job that requires button-down shirts.

But Kate will spend her time sneaking pureed spinach into pasta sauce, cinnamon in with the coffee grounds, substituting organic soups for Campbell's condensed cream of mushroom in casserole dishes. Mostly Jason won't notice, but when he does, they'll fight about it. Ann's now-single life seems extravagant, full of possibility.

• • •

The Rich Guy had Ann meet him at his house, had her walk through the garage with his four cars: a Range Rover, a Bentley, a Lexus, and a Jeep. In the kitchen, she kept thinking: *I know this kitchen.* During dinner, she remembered. The neighborhood. The house. The kitchen. They'd done the custom cabinets for the remodel—it'd been a pain-in-the-ass job. The wife finding fault with everything, sending things back, changing her mind. She'd only worked with the wife. She'd been the only contact, signed all the checks.

Over dinner, he told her he wasn't from money. The money was his wife's. He told her money didn't matter.

Over dinner, he told her it was mostly a marriage of convenience. They were mostly companions. She'd died eight months ago, stomach cancer. Their daughter—his daughter—is Emily; she's eight. One year older than Luna.

"It's too soon," Kate says, when Ann finally fills her in on the Rich Guy. Kate gives lots of advice.

"The girls get along pretty well," Ann continues. "Don't worry. I'm taking it slow."

"Uh-huh…"

"It's nice to go out with a grown-up. And the four of us go out for the most part. Most guys run the other way when they find out I have a kid."

He brings bags of hand-me-downs for Luna; they're all name brand, most with tags on.

When she doesn't have Luna for the weekend, she goes over to his house and hangs out with him and Emily. One Saturday he invites his parents for dinner, so she wears her nicest simplest chicest dress. When Emily sees her dressed up for fancy dinner, she insists on dressing up too. Ann curls her hair and puts just a dab of lip gloss on her. Emily puts on her party dress with sparkles.

She comes out to twirl for everyone and the Rich Guy groans. All dinner he grimaces. Emily smiles, baring her teeth. After the parents leave, and the kitchen is cleaned up, the custom cabinets loaded and closed whisper-silent on their custom-order European hinges, the silverware slid into the maple dovetail joint drawer boxes on full-extension, soft-close, undermount slides, she finds the Rich Guy irritably picking glitter off the chair Emily sat on for dinner. He's swearing under his breath.

"Next time," he says, "do me a favor. Don't encourage her."

• • •

"I think," she says to Kate, "I just tick a lot of boxes for him. I'm the right age, have a decent job, smart enough, good-looking enough." She continues, before Kate can interrupt, "And he wants a mother for Emily."

"Well, does he do anything more than tick a lot of boxes for you?" The line is silent.

• • •

The Fun Guy was Luna's favorite. They go on dates during the day every weekend she has Luna—to the beach, the park, Disney, anywhere kids would have fun. Ann walks behind them, carrying the bags, the folding chairs, the umbrella, dragging the cooler draped with whatever she can…trying to make as few trips as possible. Some of her favorite photos of Luna are from the time of the Fun Guy. Her little girl smiles wide, showing her crooked teeth unselfconsciously, and her lips aren't stiff like in most pictures. The wind is always blowing her hair; her clothes are always a mess and no one seems to mind.

He never seems to mind that Ann has a daughter, never seems to mind when that means she's too tired for an adult date, or they just end up ordering pizza and watching Pixar movies, half-asleep on the couch. When she starts picking up and getting ready to put Luna to bed, he helps collect toys, organizes the leftover Lego pieces, chastely kisses Ann at the door after high-fiving Luna and leaves by eight-thirty. They barely ever have sex.

He still lives at home with his parents, helping to take care of his older brother who has Down's syndrome and cerebral palsy. Once he brought his brother to the park with them, and then he had more to carry than Ann, navigating the electric chair on the crushed seashell paths when the sidewalk ended, waiting patiently for the lift gate to lower, checking the brakes. He talked to his brother the whole time, and his brother answered, in his way, bobbing his head and smiling his own wide smile, offering a clumsy high five or two. But Luna seemed a little spooked and a little jealous; she'd lost her playmate.

And that was when Ann knew it would never work. The Fun Guy needed those days with her and Luna—mostly needed those days with Luna, to be a kid, and not have to feel responsible for someone else. His parents were getting older, and he lived at home—soon he'd be a caregiver to more than just his brother. The next time there was a Thursday, and Luna was at her dad's, and they had sex, Ann tried to be her wildest, to give him as much pleasure as she could—even doing the things that always felt ridiculous, the things she and Kate laughed about guys liking, like "reverse cowgirl" (Kate always said it should be called "peripatetic frog"), but she knew she was trying too hard—performing—and that he knew it too.

When he left that night, the kiss was almost unbearably sweet. Luna really missed him.

• • •

The Nice Guy is very understanding. After a few whirlwind-can't-keep-their-hands-off-each-other dates, dates that make them late for dinner, dates that end up before dinner sweaty on the couch, pants and panties hooked on ankles, one shoe off and one shoe on, Ann tells him, "I can't keep going out Thursdays."

He nods. "Friday's I'm in a fog at work—I'm groggy. I don't feel well. I don't get any work done."

"Okay," he says, "no more Thursdays." He smiles. "I'm just happy to see you whenever I can see you."

They take it slower. They introduce the girls. His daughter is six. Luna gets to be the big girl. When he and his daughter come over for a playdate, they hang out at the pool. Luna shows off her diving, her butterfly, and her front crawl. Casey hangs on her dad's shoulder, pretending to be shy. Before she does anything in the pool, she coos, "Dadddyyy…" and he smiles.

"Casey, you can do it, sweetie." She basks under his smile, this good daddy. Her mother left, unwilling to be tied down—she was too young, she said. Or that's what the Nice Guy told Ann she said. He says that she was too immature to be a mother—that she still wanted to be a party girl. He has full custody of Casey; she sees her mother a few times a year. After a few weeks, he starts texting Thursday nights. "I'm in town," he says, "picking up a few things at Target…at Lowe's…at Publix."

"I'm tired," she texts back.

"I'm settled in for the night."

"No thanks," she replies. Firmly, she thinks.

He starts popping over. She feels bad when she sees his sweet smile at the peephole. He always brings pizza and a six-pack. Or Chinese take-out and a six-pack. Or tacos and six-pack.

They end up on the couch.

They have their first big fight about Kim Davis, the clerk in Kentucky who refuses to issue marriage licenses. He says it's not a fight—it's a little disagreement. He says they don't really disagree about much, just this one little thing.

. . .

When she tells Kate about him, Kate checks out his Facebook page when they're on the phone. "Uh-oh," Kate says, "red flag."

"What?" Ann asks.

"Did you see his cover photo?"

"Uh-huh," Ann answers. It's an American flag, soft-focus, with girls in bikinis. She was hoping Kate wouldn't notice—or wouldn't say anything.

"Red flag," Kate says—that's all she says.

Their second big fight—he corrects her, "It's a little disagreement, Ann"—comes when he quotes Rush Limbaugh, as if the man is some kind of guru.

"The thing is," Ann continues, "we don't really agree on much."

"But you're wrong, Ann," he says. It's another Thursday night. He's wheedled his way into her apartment—wheedled his way into her bed. She was planning to be eating a dinner by herself, watching some TV, enjoying some quiet on a night without Luna.

"We agree on so much." But his saying it doesn't seem to make it true, although the way he says it is so reasonable. As if to bring up the ways they disagree would be mean-spirited, especially now that his fingers are interlaced with hers and he is sweat-sheened and sloe-eyed.

Last time she talked to Kate she told her how he made reservations for them at a fancy restaurant, picked her up, ordered for her, and she felt like she was on a *real date* for once. Being wined and dined and romanced. "Red flag," Kate said.

"Dump him," Kate said when she told her about the Thursday Issue. "I've got it!" she shrieked. "Text him: 'I'm dumping you. This is for Sandra Fluke.'" Kate thinks she's so fucking hilarious sometimes.

• • •

Ann's at the bar, nursing a seltzer. She's out with some friends from work, trying to enjoy a little camaraderie, a little chitchat, without it turning into a late-night, regret-it-in-the-morning, hook-up-with-some-guy-not-worth-her-time. But here comes some guy—definitely not worth her time.

"I noticed you're not drinking," he says. *That's not even worthy of a response*, Ann thinks. Once again, she wishes she had a really withering look. Over the years, she's worked on it—always admiring those women who can deploy it like a weapon, whose faces are armor. Maybe she's getting better at it though.

He's short. And he looks like her ex-husband, who is also short. She senses he's going to try again. He inclines his head slightly toward her, raises his glass. *Oh no, he's going to try to buy her a drink.* Ann looks toward her group of friends, but they're deep in conversation—she's on her own.

"Me neither," he says, smiling a little. "I've been sober two years, seven months." Her face turns red—is she wearing some kind of label she forgot to take off? "If you're going to hang around in bars, it helps to order something that looks like a drink—

that way, people won't bother you so much…" His eyes go to his glass, which looks like a gin and tonic.

"Have them add a lime to yours," he suggests, "or get a seltzer with a shot of cranberry on top."

"Um, thanks…" and her face is bright red now, but hopefully the bar light hides it. She can feel the way sweat has broken out all over her chest, and her hands are shaking and she would really like a fuck-ing cigarette, but she'll have to go outside for that.

"I'm Mike, by the way," and he reaches out his hand, and she shakes it with her shaking hand, then blurts out, "I have to go to the bathroom," and runs.

When she tells Kate, Kate says, "That's the kind of guy you should have talked to—a Legitimately Nice Guy."

"No way," Ann says. "He was short and he looked like Greg."

• • •

The problem with the Good-in-Bed Guy is that he'll always be the Good-in-Bed Guy. He might be a lot of other things too, but whatever else they're doing— driving somewhere, or waiting in line at a movie, or lying on the beach—in the back of her head, Ann's always thinking, *he's so good in bed*. Kate can't even imagine getting past those first few months of dating—would they be grocery shopping or paying bills, and all the time she'd be thinking, *he's so good in bed*?

"Worse than that," Kate adds, "I'd always be waiting for the sex to go downhill. It can't stay like that—right?"

"Does that happen?" Ann asks. "Do people marry the Good-in-Bed Guy?" But neither of them have any idea—they haven't heard of such a thing. Maybe people who do don't ever talk about it. More likely it never happens.

Half the time, the Good-in-Bed Guy is also the Asshole. Like the Really Good Looking Guy, he knows it. Kate says you can never trust a Really Good Looking Guy either—they never develop any of their other traits. She prefers the overweight guys, the balding guys, even the guy whose shoulder hair was so thick his shirts hovered a good inch and a half above the curve of skin. Those guys had to work for it a little bit—they were smart, or interesting, or kind.

"I'll admit it," Kate says, "I objectify the Good-in-Bed Guy—that's all he ever is. I don't think I could take him seriously."

"What about—?"

"Exactly. Never would have worked." Kate manages the Good-in-Bed Guy by ensuring finite deadlines, or creating them. There was the study-abroad boyfriend who was someone else's husband, and besides she was going back to the States. There was the on-again off-again college boyfriend, but even their sexual chemistry couldn't overcome the national debates preceding the general election. In fact, Kate manages everything by ensuring finite deadlines, or creating them. That, and her withering look.

When she was giving Ann the play by play about the study-abroad boyfriend, how she didn't even need to be on top, how everything he did was successful, even from behind, Ann stopped her, "Riding high or low?" Kate gave her the withering look. When Ann was explaining the most recent Good-in-Bed Guy, and some magic trick he did with his fingers while he was already inside her, they were at the local bar, but it was a Tuesday and mostly deserted. Kate grabbed the sugar packets, the squeeze bottles of ketchup and mustard, salt and pepper shakers, drink stirrers and a cardboard coaster, pushed them toward Kate across the curved edge of the bar.

"Demonstrate," she said, nodding her head, chin jutting forward and lifted at the pile of materials between them.

"What?" Ann asked, laughing, picking up the squeeze mustard—wondering what that could possibly signify. Is she the mustard bottle?

"Create a diagram." After much research, Ann and Kate have determined the Good-In-Bed Guy is nontransferable, as are his moves.

• • •

There was the love letter of the old Beloved—gifted from Kate to Ann, as an offer of pleasure. But he provided no pleasure to Ann. And Kate misjudged her feelings, realized she still had some, and that the old Beloved wasn't yet wholly separate, free to give. And then he decided he had feelings too—for Ann.

There is the love letter sent and re-sent by Ann, whereby she pretends to forget how Kate betrayed her once, unforgivably. And Kate appreciates this, so only brings it up often.

And there are all the things they haven't spoken of—until some missent love-letter of a look, in the dim bar light.

TWELVE
PROGRESS

Where the few billboards are planted like exotic blooms rooted in fields of yellowed grass and thistle, the paint blistered, advertising local businesses or an occasional local opinion in too-small type, not readable even at the speed cars pass here. Off the county highways named with double letters, off the state highways named with double digits, far from the interstates where cars pass by at unimaginable speeds and the billboards are illuminated in LED lights, with smart screens that change their messages every few car lengths.

Here are the towns half-forgotten, cut off, sequestered, where the babies are born covered in fine gray down, smooth watered silk, like a row of thread spools in Copenhagen, Nickel and Steel, all the colors you'd use for quilting a clear night sky or the layers of lake over a stone bottom. Their eyelashes rest easy on this furred skin, and the mothers know their babies to be beautiful. They pet their sealbabies, holding them huddled in layers of skin and fur, warmed through winter, slickened and curved like a wish made flesh.

Their mothers think them lovely, these natural swimmers, these perfect epitomes of grace, and know that as they age their downed skin thins, becoming paler, until by school age they only wear a light layer of silver glint on their limbs, the parts of their faces where the sun touches. But with the wiring of the county, some project for the rural poor, they come to know that other babies are born pink already, sunburned and pinched, without the calm mien of the sealbabies. And when the improvements continue, a literacy project for the library, the construction of a rural clinic, they become afraid, swaddling their babies tighter, covering their lovely starlight skins from the inevitable strangers in town, hiding this beauty from outsiders.

But the new doctor catches sight, after months of agitating for prenatal care, for a new ob-gyn suite, of one of the young mother's treasures she's been keeping. He prescribes treatments, deaf to pleas, discovers a treasure trove of genetic mutations, the sort of thing that could make a person famous, feather a nest with accolades and citations for years to come. He discovers the secret swimming hole in the woods, fed by ground spring, the last safety of mothers letting their babies be their babies before he prescribes best-selling advice and self-help books, telling these women to resist their impulses, to curb their animals, to put on their clothes and stop dropping their poor sick babies into the water hole like dumplings into hot soup. Cover your nakedness, women; cover the bodies of your malformed children, all big dark eyes and long lashes, looking too long with too much intent.

And the treatments, pills and salves, unctions and ointments, worked so well the babies became sunburned pink, denuded and pinched, lost the will to swim, helpless by land and by sea. The mothers were new mothers all over again; not knowing how to care for these new beasts—all squalling desire, and no self-soothe. Their skin blistered and raged, drying and scaling in even the softest breeze. The doctor prescribed new creams to treat the uncovered skin, mottled and rash-red, pained and hot to the touch.

Drop a snake into this island ecosystem. The stowaway of wheel well, curved around landing gear. But imagine before that: the exotic plumage, the exquisite adaptations. If no one teaches you what beauty should be, you know it yourself. If no one shows you what pleasure is, you find it yourself.

The mothers wanted their sealbabies back. They asked the Nonnas, but they had no answers: they told the stories of the time the first group of men came to town, and they had to learn to live apart, two by two, instead of sisters with sisters, like it used to be. That was the beginning of the sealbabies, the Nonnas said. You lose something, you get something. Progress does what it does; that's the way with it, they say—pointing across the field where someone was building a tower.

"What's that?" one of the children asks, and in this light she still shines, silver-glint. Her mother shifts a baby hip to hip, bouncing and jostling, trying to appease the pink-curdled anger growing in her baby's face.

"A cell tower," the mother says, sighing, long shadows beneath her eyes. The child wants to ask more questions, but doesn't have the language to ask, quiver of silky down lip, big eyes raised to the sky.

THIRTEEN

A LOVE LETTER

It is summer in Wisconsin, and the long late evening light has faded. They are in Ann's car. She has picked Kate up from work, and they probably made two or three circles around the local Hardee's where the cute boy Ann likes works, finally ordering through the drive-through, the greasy bags of fries and burgers cooling in the backseat. They have stopped by Kate's father's house, snuck into the back basement, past the piles of half-unfinished projects, the piles of left-behind treasures of childhood toys and discarded outgrown clothes, a box or two still belonging to Kate's mother, forgotten and dust-covered, to liberate a can of spray-paint: Gold Krylon.

They are sixteen or seventeen, a few summers past the summer of the Castle by the Sea, a few summers before the college and Study Abroad adventures. They drive too fast down residential streets, and Ann smiles her sweet I'm-from-out-of-town smile and the local police officer gives them a warning and tells them to be more careful and they take off again into the night.

They drive the back road that skirts the mill-pond where you slow to watch the snapping turtles cross the narrow asphalt between the flooded fields and ponds; they remember trying to help a big she-snapper, laughing and scared as her neck extended as long as her body, biting the tree branch, so they could drag her to the other side, out of the road. As they drove away, she turned around in the shoulder and headed back across. But tonight, they are headed to the ninety-degree bend beyond, the abandoned trestle bridge over the concrete underpass known as Graffiti Bridge.

And they are giggling wordlessly, the car lights extinguished, Ann's Honda nestled into the ditch, Kate making large letters in the dark, when a solitary flashlight comes bobbing out of the field.

"Hey!" a bodiless voice yells. "What the hell are you doing?" Ann is immediately at Kate's side, and Kate has partially obscured the Krylon can behind her body, and they are silent except for laughter that cannot be contained. Even the peepers go quiet.

"I said," the voice continues, angry, "what are you girls doing?" They cannot see who is speaking, but it is a man, older, and the penumbra of the flashlight fully obscures him, fully blinds them.

"What's your name?" he asks, focusing the light on Kate. Ann is there, preparing, thinking of the fake name she will give when he turns to her, but Kate answers quick.

"Kate Donovan, D-O-N-O-V-A-N."

"Well, you're trespassing and damaging my property," the voice says, "and I'm calling the police." The voice is exasperated.

"Okay," Kate says. That's all she says.

"You kids come out here all the time, writing your dirty words on my property—you think it's funny I bet," and maybe he can see Kate squeeze Ann's hand, and the pressure of their hands together stifle the laugh in both of them threatening to break free.

"Well, I'm calling the cops. This is my property, and I'm sick of this bullshit. This vandalism—I'm goddamned sick of it." He seems to have forgotten to ask Ann's name, and he doesn't seem to be moving, not to make a call, not to confirm Kate's name.

"What the hell did you write anyway?" he asks, and the flashlight scans the wall behind them, their new gold letters standing out in a palimpsest of letters and colors layered year upon year. The light catches the metallic in their letters, Kate's shaky, drawn-in-the-dark characters, only the final curve of the last "n" unfinished.

"Kate loves Ann," Kate answers.

• • •

Luna will love this story and beg to be told it again and again. One summer they will take her to Graffiti Bridge to see if their love letter is still there. "No," they tell her, he didn't call the police. When she asks why they gave their real names, Kate tells her, *because it's important to tell the truth.*

"It wasn't his property anyway," Kate says. "It's an old railroad bridge. Those are public property—he was just the neighbor."

They each think maybe they can see a glitter of gold here and there, but the bridge has been painted many times—cans and cans of color, messages of love, tags that declare to the world, *I Was Here*, and more simply, *I Exist*, and the simplest of all: *I*.

EPILOGUE
QUARTERS

Ice from the ice machine sounds one way in cubes, another when crushed. Deeper sounds into pint glasses or tallboys, squat sounds into short glasses, the kind that hold martinis or liquor straight. Whether it's the first or a refill affects, subtly, the wind chime music of ice and glass and alcohol. And it sounds one way when you're in the room. And another when you're in the next room, listening. And another when you're in bed, trying to sleep, but nowhere near sleep. And another wholly when you're asleep but awoken by the familiar sound. A music box of sorts—percussive and atonal, regular as a reverse sleep machine.

• • •

Her mommy's Lonely smells sweet and makes music. Her daddy's Lonely sounds like whispers and giggles in the hallway when she's already in bed with lots of Daddy's voice saying "shush" and "be quiet" in his pretend-angry voice.

At her mommy's house, Luna only hears the Lonely after bedtime, when she's snuggled in her covers and the nightlight is on, but her mommy's phone starts making its ping sounds, so she knows people are talking to her mommy but not really talking. Sometimes she hears just her mommy's voice talking to someone on the phone but she can't tell who she's talking to most of the time, unless it's Aunt Kate. When Mommy is talking to Aunt Kate, Mommy says, "Kaaaate…" stretching out the middle of Aunt Kate's name and then she knows that Mommy is talking about something serious: that she's had a bad day at work, or that she's worried about something, and sometimes Luna's worried that she's worried about her. There's also lots of laughing and most of it sounds like real laughing, and lots of being quiet because Aunt Kate talks a lot.

At her daddy's house, she only hears the Lonely a long time after her bedtime, when she wakes up still sleepy and she knows her daddy has called one of his friends to come over and help him not be lonely. She falls back asleep and in the morning only her daddy is there so she doesn't know who was the giggling-whisper voice and she knows not to ask her daddy because then she'll see the lonely on his face that he tries to hide with the pretend-angry. He'll say things like, "Hurry up and eat your cereal," or, "Hurry up, we're going to be late for school" or he'll pretend he didn't hear her and go out to the garage and start loading the car.

Daddy has lots of cars—the regular car, and the work truck, and the junker car that he's always working on that Luna calls the rat car, and sometimes when he's working on the junker car, lying on the garage floor with only his feet sticking out, he'll start singing and she'll start singing too, quietly, and they'll both be singing silly songs about nothing and then there's no Lonely in the garage at all.

Sometimes she'll hear the same whisper-voice again and again and then Daddy will ask if she wants to meet one of his friends and she won't answer but he knows that she does so his friend will come over for dinner or they'll go out to Chili's where she likes to eat fries and Daddy's friend will talk to her in a voice different than the whisper-voice and try to be her friend too.

When Mommy has a new friend she usually gets to meet his daughter too, and sometimes they are friends then and they go to the park or the beach or swimming at the pool, and once they went to Disney all together. She can feel the way Mommy watches her friend and his daughter and she can feel the way he watches Mommy and her and then the Lonely feels different, but it's still there. She thinks everyone grown-up has their own Lonely; she thinks when she grows up she'll have her own Lonely too.

Sometimes they Skype with Aunt Kate and Mommy and Aunt Kate think they are very smart and if they talk a certain way—using letters instead of names, using big words instead of little words— that she won't know what they're talking about.

But she knows that words and names are only half of what grown-ups say when they say what they're saying and she knows most of what they're saying anyway. Lots of times they talk about Daddy and his friends or Mommy and her friends or Luna and whether she's still getting extra help at school with Mrs. Schwartz at the special-help reading table or whether Grandma Polly or Grandpa Doug are feeling any better and Luna knows that they are talking about serious grown-up stuff and she listens very closely and later she mostly figures it out.

One time when Aunt Kate was visiting, and she and Mommy were getting ready to go out, Aunt Kate tried on every dress in her suitcase and even tried on some of Mommy's clothes too, but she wasn't happy with anything, and she curled her hair then brushed it straight and had Mommy do her makeup but she still wasn't happy and every time she looked in the mirror she took a big breath, then blew it all out, but no matter what she did she couldn't look taller and every time Mommy stood next to her in the mirror and smiled, Aunt Kate's eyes slid to the sides to look at her.

"Now you know how it feels," Luna said to Aunt Kate, and Aunt Kate's mouth dropped open and she laughed one of her big Aunt Kate laughs and picked Luna up and rolled around on the bed, hugging her, and then when they went out later her hair was still messed up from playing with Luna but Aunt Kate didn't seem to mind anymore.

Mommy had laughed too, but turned to Aunt Kate and said, quiet, "I told you she listens to us."

When they Skype with Aunt Kate, Aunt Kate makes lots of jokes and laughs a lot, even when Mommy looks upset or is using letters and big words. That's how Aunt Kate's Lonely sounds.

Sometimes after she meets one of Daddy's friends at Chili's, and then Daddy's friend starts staying at the house and pouring her cereal in the morning, she starts thinking of Daddy's friend as her friend too. Then she starts telling Aunt Kate that she has a new dog, or a new cat, or a dog and cat, because they moved into Daddy's house with Daddy's friend. Once a friend named Heather lived with them for a few months, and she brought a dog named Muffin. The next time Luna Skyped with Aunt Kate she told her that she had a new dog named Muffin and Mommy shook her head a little to Aunt Kate but Luna saw it too.

• • •

And most of Daddy's friends were nice to her, even if after a while Daddy wasn't so nice to them anymore. Heather stayed with them the longest, and she would braid Luna's hair, or paint her toenails with glitter paint if she was painting her own, and sometimes on Saturdays if Daddy had to work they'd go to the thrifty stores and buy twirly skirts that smelled bad until they brought them home and washed them. Then Luna would dress-up dress up and they would all go out to Chili's for french fries.

•••

When Luna walked into her room her piggy bank was on her dresser, not her table, and when she picked it up it felt mostly empty. Not heavy like it did when it was full of all the quarters and pennies and nickels and dimes that she'd been putting into it since Mommy brought it back from her trip to Mexico with Aunt Kate when she was five and Mommy said she was too little to go and besides it was a grown-up trip.

She went into the kitchen and Daddy was drinking from a can of beer and Heather was standing at the stove stirring taco meat for dinner.

"Daddy," she said, her pouty bottom lip out a little (Daddy hates when she sticks her pouty bottom lip out), "Daddy…" and then she didn't say anything else but held out her piggy bank.

Heather didn't turn around, but stood at the stove, stirring the taco meat that already smelled good.

"What?" Daddy said in his I-just-got-home-from-work-and-I'm-tired voice as he set down the beer and took the piggy bank.

"It's all gone," she whispered.

"What?" he said, but this time different, like he didn't hear her.

"Gone," she said, louder, with her pouty bottom lip out. She pointed at the piggy bank.

Daddy's eyes slid slow, out of the corners, to the piggy bank in his hands, to Heather stirring the taco meat on the stove, back to Luna standing there with her pouty bottom lip and back to Heather at the stove.

"Heather?" And now Daddy's voice was really angry, but Heather kept stirring and didn't turn around. She pointed with the plastic spoon to the six-pack sitting on the counter, one of its plastic loops empty and stretched out, the two packs of Marlboro mediums.

"I was a little short," Heather said to the taco meat, not turning around.

"Luna, go to your room," Daddy said, quiet. His quiet voice was even worse than his angry voice and she ran to her room, slamming the door. Slamming the door wasn't allowed, but she heard more slamming doors and more angry voice, Daddy's voice and Heather's voice, and then car doors, and then driving away.

She and Daddy ate tacos later and there were lots of leftovers because Heather wasn't there and Muffin wasn't there and Daddy threw all the rest of the taco meat in the garbage and all the taco shells because he said *the goddamn things would go stale by tomorrow* but he put the cheese in a zipper bag and put that back in the refrigerator.

She went to her mommy's the next day and the next day but when she went back to her daddy's her piggy bank was back on the table and next to it was a whole roll of quarters like the kind they got when they went to laundromat to do clothes.

She sat on her bed putting the quarters into her piggy bank one by one, listening to the thunks. Mommy said money is dirty and you have to wash your hands after touching it, but Luna wasn't going to wash her hands. Before she put the last quarter into the piggy bank, she put it in her mouth, feeling the heavy on her tongue. She held it against her pouty lip until it got warm, twirling the ridges against her mouth, feeling the sharp and the metal and the dirty she wasn't supposed to touch. And Daddy didn't ever mention the quarters and she didn't either, but the next time they went to the laundromat because *the goddamned washer was still broken*, he handed her the whole roll of quarters and let her put them into every machine. While their clothes were spinning spinning in the dryers, they played all the games, even the Crane game, which was *a racket* and *no one ever won at*, and even though there was no one else in the whole place, she knew the Lonely was there with them.

AUTHOR'S ACKNOWLEDGMENTS

Thank you to *Ginosko Literary Review*, where an earlier version of "Quarters" appeared.

Thanks to the smart and creative women who were early readers of these stories: Jen Escher (who encouraged my first efforts at fiction, offering suggestions along the way), Kari Meyer (who pretended the characters were real people, getting upset on their behalf), and Jennifer D. Sims (for editing, argument, and constant conversation).

Thank you to John for sitting next to me on the couch when I can't—or won't—get off the computer, always kissing me good-night and good-bye, and listening when I go on and on.

Lastly, Carmen: this is a love letter to you—my best friend, my almost-sister. If the ways you enrich my life were measured in words, this would be an epic.

ABOUT THE AUTHOR

C. Kubasta writes poetry, fragments, prose, and occasional reviews and columns. Her poetry book *All Beautiful & Useless* (BlazeVOX, 2015) explored growing up a girl in rural Wisconsin; her second poetry collection, *Of Covenants*, released from Whitepoint Press in 2017. She lives, writes, and teaches in Wisconsin, where she is often inspired by the rural, the bodies we inhabit, the subtexts of our relationships and our selves. For each major publication, she celebrates with a new tattoo; someday she hopes to be completely sleeved— her skin a labyrinth of signifiers, utterly opaque. Find her at *www.ckubasta.com* and follow her @CKubastathePoet.